Contents

YORK NOTES

General Editors: Professor A.N. Jeffares (*University of Stirling*) & Professor Suheil Bushrui (*American University of Beirut*)

Emily Brontë

WUTHERING HEIGHTS

Notes by Angela Smith

MA (BIRMINGHAM) M LITT (CAMBRIDGE)
Lecturer in English Studies, University of Stirling

LONGMAN
YORK PRESS

YORK PRESS
Immeuble Esseily, Place Riad Solh, Beirut.

LONGMAN GROUP UK LIMITED
Longman House, Burnt Mill, Harlow,
Essex CM20 2JE, England
Associated companies, branches and representatives
throughout the world

© Librairie du Liban 1980

First published 1980
Ninth impression 1990

ISBN 0-582-02324-6

Produced by Longman Group (FE) Ltd.
Printed in Hong Kong

Part 1

Introduction

The life of Emily Brontë

When she was twenty, Charlotte Brontë, Emily's older sister, wrote to the Poet Laureate, Robert Southey, sending him some of her poems and asking his advice. His reply contained the following paragraph:

> Literature cannot be the business of a woman's life, and it ought not to be. The more she is engaged in her proper duties, the less leisure she will have for it, even as an accomplishment and a recreation. To those duties you have not yet been called, and when you are you will be less eager for celebrity. You will not seek in imagination for excitement, of which the vicissitudes of this life . . . will bring with them but too much.*

Both Charlotte Brontë and her biographer, Elizabeth Gaskell, considered this 'admirable' advice although both were distinguished novelists. A glimpse that Mrs Gaskell gives us of the Brontës' domestic routine gives an insight into the life of a woman who was also a writer in the middle of the nineteenth century in England.

> It was Emily who made all the bread for the family; and anyone passing by the kitchen door might have seen her studying German out of an open book, propped up before her, as she kneaded the dough; but no study, however interesting, interfered with the goodness of the bread, which was always light and excellent.†

These three sensitive and intelligent women seem to have agreed that their responsibility to their families had higher priority than the fulfilment of their creative imagination.

> When a man becomes an author, it is probably merely a change of employment to him . . . But no other can take up the quiet regular duties of the daughter, the wife, or the mother, as well as she whom God has appointed to fill that particular place: a woman's principal work in life is hardly left to her own choice; nor can she drop the domestic charges devolving on her as an individual, for the exercise of the most splendid talents that were ever bestowed.‡

The Life of Charlotte Brontë by Elizabeth Gaskell, London, 1857, Chapter 8
†Gaskell, Chapter 8
‡Gaskell, Chapter 16

The Brontë sisters had lived from infancy with the conventional belief that all educational advantages must be given to sons rather than daughters; there were five girls and one boy in their family.

Emily Brontë was born on 30 July 1818 at Thornton in Yorkshire. She had three older sisters, Maria, Elizabeth, and Charlotte, and a brother, Branwell; her younger sister, Anne, was born in 1820. Her father was a clergyman of the Church of England who moved with his family from Thornton to Haworth, also in Yorkshire, soon after Anne's birth. Te parsonage, where he was to remain for the rest of his long life, was a stone house built at the summit of a steep village street overlooking the graveyard. Beyond it were, and still are, paths to the moors, high exposed stretches of country with occasional outcrops of rock, covered with heather and interlaced with small streams; from her earliest years Emily Brontë went for walks on the moors with her brother and sisters. Her mother became ill with cancer soon after the family moved to Haworth and died in 1821 when she was thirty-nine.

Mr Brontë taught his son himself but in 1824 he sent Maria, Elizabeth, Charlotte and Emily to a school for the daughters of clergy at Cowan Bridge, fifty miles from Haworth. What kind of experience it provided for at least one of its pupils can be deduced from Charlotte's account of Lowood in *Jane Eyre*. The founder of the school believed in harsh discipline and unremitting work; the pupils' food was appallingly bad and they suffered from cold throughout the winter. As a result both Maria and Elizabeth died of tuberculosis in the spring of 1825, at which time there was also an outbreak of typhoid fever at the school. Charlotte and Emily were taken home by their father, where Emily formed a particularly close relationship with Anne that lasted throughout their lives.

At home they virtually educated themselves by reading avidly whatever they could. Their father's lively interest in politics, art and literature and his discussions with their Aunt Branwell, who had come to care for them after their mother's death, stimulated their interest to such an extent that they created imaginary worlds, fusing fantasy and reality in an extraordinary way. Charlotte wrote in her account of the year 1829:

> Papa bought Branwell some wooden soldiers at Leeds; when papa came home it was night, and we were in bed, so next morning Branwell came to our door with a box of soldiers. Emily and I jumped out of bed, and I snatched up one and exclaimed, 'This is the Duke of Wellington! This shall be the Duke!' . . . Branwell chose his and called him 'Buonaparte'.*

These soldiers had imaginary adventures in a landscape that was derived

*Quoted in Gaskell, Chapter 5

from the *Arabian Nights* and their knowledge of the geography of Africa. Many of their 'plays' were written down in tiny writing and bound into miniature magazines. Emily and Anne developed their own fantasy world, Gondal, which was supposed to be an island in the North Pacific, though its climate resembled that of Yorkshire. They began writing about it in 1831 when Charlotte went away to school; the saga was in both prose and verse, though only the poems are extant, and was continued until shortly before Emily's death in 1848. Most of Emily's poetry seems to have been written for her Gondal saga, though it may also reflect her own experience.

She went to school when she was seventeen but pined so quickly for home that she was allowed to return there. However in 1837 she became a teacher near Halifax for a short time, as all three sisters had to earn their livings to spare such money as there was for Branwell's education. They thought of setting up a school together but decided that they should improve their own education first, so Emily and Charlotte went as pupils to the Pensionnat Héger in Brussels early in 1842 but only remained until November as their aunt died on 29 October. Charlotte returned to Brussels but Emily stayed at home as housekeeper for her father. When Charlotte came home in 1844 the three sisters attempted to start a school for girls, offering French, German, Latin, music and drawing as well as the usual academic subjects, but no pupils were forthcoming.

Their greatest trial at this time was the degenerate behaviour of the brother for whom they had sacrificed their own opportunities. He fulfilled none of his early promise and became addicted to drink and opium, unable to earn his living. However, in the autumn of 1845, Charlotte discovered notebooks containing Emily's poems, and was so impressed with their originality that she persuaded her sisters that they should try to publish their poems under the pseudonyms Currer, Ellis and Acton Bell. The book came out in May 1846, with the authors contributing towards the cost of publication. Meanwhile the sisters were writing their first novels; *Wuthering Heights* was probably started in October 1845. It was accepted for publication with Anne's novel *Agnes Grey* in July 1847 and published in December.

Branwell's health was becoming worse and he died in September 1848, leaving his sisters to lament that their 'pride and hope' had left nothing but 'a bitterness of pity' about 'the emptiness of his whole existence'.* Emily caught a cold at Branwell's funeral which developed into tuberculosis. She refused any medical aid and forced herself to continue with her normal household duties until the day of her death, 19 December 1848. Charlotte described her death in the biographical

*Written by Charlotte Brontë in a letter to W. S. Williams, quoted as a footnote in the Haworth edition of *The Life of Charlotte Brontë*, London, 1905, to Chapter 16

notice she added to the 1850 edition of *Wuthering Heights*:

> Never in all her life had she lingered over any task that lay before her, and she did not linger now. She sank rapidly. She made haste to leave us. Yet, while physically she perished, mentally, she grew stronger than we had yet known her. Day by day, when I saw with what a front she met suffering, I looked on her with an anguish of wonder and love. I have seen nothing like it; but, indeed, I have never seen her parallel in anything. Stronger than a man, simpler than a child, her nature stood alone. The awful point was, that, while full of ruth for others, on herself she had no pity; the spirit was inexorable to the flesh; from the trembling hand, the unnerved limbs, the faded eyes, the same service was exacted as they had rendered in health. To stand by and witness this, and not dare to remonstrate, was a pain no words can render.

The contemporary reception of the novel

Charlotte Brontë also felt compelled in 1850 to write a defence of *Wuthering Heights*, feeling that it had been misunderstood, though its reception was not entirely unfavourable. Its power and strangeness were recognised by most reviewers; Sydney Dobell in the *Palladium* for September 1850 described Catherine Earnshaw as 'so wonderfully fresh, so fearfully natural', the *Examiner* for 8 January 1848 said the book had 'considerable power', and other reviewers wrote of it as the product of 'a mind of limited experience, but of original energy, and of a singular and distinctive cast* showing 'more genius, in the highest sense of the word, than you will find in a thousand novels'.† Generally, however, most reviewers agreed with the critic of the *North American Review* for October 1848 when he wrote that 'the power evinced in *Wuthering Heights* is power thrown away. Nightmares and dreams, through which devils dance and wolves howl, make bad novels.'

Modern readers may feel that Charlotte was too defensive about *Wuthering Heights* because she herself did not fully understand it. She apologised for the gloom in the novel:

> Having formed these beings, she [Emily] did not know what she had done. If the auditor of her work, when read in manuscript, shuddered under the grinding influence of natures so relentless and implacable, of spirits so lost and fallen; if it was complained that the mere hearing of certain vivid and fearful scenes banished sleep by night, and disturbed mental peace by day, Ellis Bell would wonder what was meant, and suspect the complainant of affectation.‡

Britannia, 15 January 1848
†*Leader*, 28 December 1850 (a review possibly written by G. H. Lewes)
‡Preface to the 1850 edition of *Wuthering Heights*

She was frightened by the characterisation of Heathcliff; again her interpretation of his character may seem unrecognisable to a modern reader:

> Heathcliff betrays one solitary human feeling, and that is *not* his love for Catherine; which is a sentiment fierce and inhuman . . . the single link that connects Heathcliff with humanity is his rudely confessed regard for Hareton Earnshaw – the young man whom he has ruined; and then his half-implied esteem for Nelly Dean. These solitary traits omitted, we should say he was child neither of Lascar nor gypsy, but a man's shape animated by demon life – a Ghoul – an Afreet.
>
> Whether it is right or advisable to create things like Heathcliff, I do not know: I scarcely think it is.

To understand the unconventionality of the Brontës' novels, and Charlotte's fear that what they had created might be immoral, we need to take into account Mrs Gaskell's opinion:

> She was invariably shocked and distressed when she heard of any disapproval of *Jane Eyre* on the ground above mentioned. Some one said to her in London, 'You know you and I, Miss Brontë, have both written naughty books!' She dwelt much on this . . . I do not deny, for myself, the existence of coarseness here and there in her works, otherwise so entirely noble.*

If such an intelligent and sympathetic critic could think *Jane Eyre's* honesty 'coarse', *Wuthering Heights* must indeed have seemed barbaric to most ordinary Victorian readers.

Yorkshire

There is of course a deliberate element of barbarism in *Wuthering Heights* which may seem as unrealistic to the modern reader as it could have to the Victorian reader. A reviewer writing in London in 1847, found Emily Brontë's depiction of life in Yorkshire hard to believe. Mrs Gaskell, herself a native of the south of England, felt she had to describe to her contemporaries in her *Life of Charlotte Brontë* what Yorkshire people were like, almost as if she were describing a foreign country. She includes anecdotes about landowners living in houses similar to Wuthering Heights who have echoes of Hindley and Heathcliff about them.

> His great amusement and occupation had been cock-fighting. When he was confined to his chamber with what he knew would be his last illness, he had his cocks brought up there, and watched the bloody

*Gaskell, Chapter 26

battle from his bed. As his mortal disease increased, and it became impossible for him to turn so as to follow the combat, he had looking-glasses arranged in such a manner, around and above him, as he lay, that he could still see the cocks fighting. And in this manner he died.*

Haworth itself was an insanitary and gloomy place; it is not surprising or incredible that there are so many untimely deaths in the Brontës' novels when one reads Mrs Gaskell's account of life in Haworth. The graveyard stood at the top of the village, above all the houses including the parsonage, poisoning the water-springs which then trickled down to the pumps where villagers drew their water. As a result there were frequent outbreaks of typhoid and other fevers.

In its insanitary qualities Haworth did not differ from other parts of Britain, as we can tell from reading Dickens's *Bleak House* or recalling the outbreaks of cholera and typhoid in mid-Victorian England. In other respects, however, Mrs Gaskell's account of life in Yorkshire would have seemed as outlandish to a reader in the south of England as *Wuthering Heights* itself, as Yorkshire seems to Lockwood in the novel. It was an inaccessible part of England, isolated by snow in winter; the railway reached Keighley, the nearest town to Haworth, in 1847 but no track was laid to Haworth until 1864. Certainly Yorkshire was very much a part of the industrial revolution and there were mills and factories in or around Haworth, but these seem to have contributed to the sense of bleakness that visitors from the south felt there.

> The rain ceased, and the day was just suited to the scenery – wild and chill – with great masses of cloud glooming over the moors, and here and there a ray of sunshine . . . darting down into some deep glen, lighting up the tall chimney, or glistening on the windows and wet roof of the mill which lies couching in the bottom. The country got wilder and wilder as we approached Haworth; for the last four miles we were ascending a huge moor, at the very top of which lies the dreary, black-looking village of Haworth. The village street itself is one of the steepest hills I have ever seen . . . the clergyman's house, we were told, was at the top of the churchyard. So through that we went – a dreary, dreary place, literally *paved* with rain-blackened tombstones, and all on the slope.†

The people who lived in these Yorkshire villages were, like Ellen Dean, superstitious; Mrs Gaskell suggests the stories that Tabby, the Brontës' servant, who was fifty-four when she came to help to look after the children, must have told them:

> Tabby had lived in Haworth in the days when the pack-horses went through once a week, with their tinkling bells and gay worsted

*Gaskell, Chapter 2
†Gaskell, Chapter 22

adornment, carrying the produce of the country from Keighley over the hills to Colne and Burnley. What is more, she had known the 'bottom', or valley, in those primitive days when the fairies frequented the margin of the 'beck' on moonlight nights, and had known folk who had seen them. But that was when there were no mills in the valleys, and when all the wool-spinning was done by hand in the farmhouse round. 'It wur the factories as had driven 'em away,' she said.*

It is perhaps significant that the main part of *Wuthering Heights* is set at the time when Tabby was young, between 1775 and 1785.

Tabby was a Methodist, and would also have told the children of local folk-heroes like the Reverend William Grimshaw, who declared to his servant in 1744 that he had 'had a glorious vision from the third heaven'† and from then on devoted himself to reclaiming the souls of his parishioners in Haworth. There was a story that he tried in every way he could to put a stop to Haworth horse races, and when he failed he prayed for torrential rain. Immediately such floods of rain fell that the races had to be abandoned and were never resumed. When he died, ministering to his parish during a cholera epidemic, his body was carried ten miles over the moors to be buried beside his wife's, in accordance with his own instructions.

Reading and romanticism

These folk traditions fused in the Brontës' imagination with their reading. Their aunt, also a Methodist, encouraged them to read Methodist literature which Charlotte Brontë described later as 'mad Methodist Magazines, full of miracles and apparitions, of preternatural warnings, ominous dreams, and frenzied fanaticism.'‡ They were devoted admirers of Scott and Byron, of Aesop's *Fables* and *The Arabian Nights*. Their reading and Tabby's stories fostered a fascination with the superhuman and the supernatural; Gondal, the imaginary world about which Emily wrote, was full of wild love and isolation, remorse and cruelty. There are echoes of Wordsworth, whom they also read, in both *Wuthering Heights* and the poems; the release from his physical self through nature which Wordsworth describes in *The Prelude* is similar to Emily Brontë's poem 'I'm happiest when most away'. The beginning of Volume II Chapter 11 of *Wuthering Heights* reminds the reader of Wordsworth's evocation of the influence of his childhood on an adult's feelings in *The Prelude* and elsewhere.

Emily Brontë's is a romantic imagination. Heathcliff has much in common with the Byronic hero who was often a rebel against moral as well as social law, often of mysterious origin, and was isolated in some way from those around him. The expression of the consuming intensity of the love between Heathcliff and Catherine is comparable to poems by Shelley and Byron, and Emily Brontë's interest in the supernatural and in dreams is characteristically romantic. She invests the landscape of the novel with moral and emotional significance as Wordsworth does, and, like Wordsworth and Blake, she is preoccupied with childhood: the link between Heathcliff and Catherine was forged in childhood and conditions the way they behave as adults.

She was no more out of touch, however, with the realities of the contemporary world than she was with those of domestic life. The family took, read, and discussed two newspapers with opposing political views, and also saw *Blackwood's Magazine*. Mr Brontë was always interested in politics. The romanticism of *Wuthering Heights* is balanced and controlled by an awareness of the real world with its financial pressures, and domestic and social responsibilities; the kind of balance that Scott achieved in *The Heart of Midlothian*. The mixture of common sense and superstition in Jeannie Deans may have influenced the creation of Ellen Dean.

A note on the text

The manuscript of *Wuthering Heights* was accepted by T. C. Newby sometime in 1847 and was published by 14 December of that year. It was published as a three-volume edition, with *Wuthering Heights* as the first two volumes and Anne's *Agnes Grey* as the third. Two hundred and fifty copies were printed and the authors had to contribute fifty pounds towards the cost. Newby was an inefficient publisher and the first edition is full of short paragraphs, meaningless commas, dashes, exclamation marks and incorrectly placed question marks. It is difficult for a modern editor to decide how many of these features were in Emily Brontë's original manuscript, particularly as little else that she wrote in prose survives; there are no stories, only one or two letters and essays. The editors of the Clarendon edition assume that the paragraphing was her own and that her rather erratic punctuation found its way uncorrected into the first edition.

In 1850 Charlotte Brontë prepared the second edition for her own publishers, Smith, Elder and Company, modifying the text considerably. She ran short paragraphs together, altered the punctuation, and simplified Joseph's dialect. This edition was accompanied by a biographical note and a preface by Charlotte. There was a similar edition in 1858.

In 1851 there was a Continental edition similar to the 1850 British one; this was published by Bernhard Tauchnitz in Leipzig. In 1848 the first American edition was published without *Agnes Grey*; the two novels were together in all the editions mentioned above. *Wuthering Heights* was published by Harper and Brothers of New York and the title page stated that it was 'A Novel by the Author of *Jane Eyre*'; the 1857 edition from the same publishers rectified this to 'A Novel by Ellis Bell'.

The best modern edition is that edited by Hilda Marsden and Ian Jack, Clarendon Press, Oxford, 1976.

Part 2

Summaries
of WUTHERING HEIGHTS

A general summary

In 1801 Mr Lockwood rents Thrushcross Grange, an elegant country house at Gimmerton in Yorkshire; his landlord, Heathcliff, a surly man, lives at Wuthering Heights, an upland farm. Lockwood is snow-bound on a visit to the Heights and has to stay the night; he dreams that he sees a child knocking at his window and saying that her name is Catherine Linton and she has been a waif for twenty years. After he gets home his housekeeper, Ellen Dean, tells him the story of the Earnshaw family at the Heights where she was brought up. The Earnshaws had two children, Hindley and Catherine, and after a visit to Liverpool Mr Earnshaw brought home a destitute child, about the same age as Catherine, whom they called Heathcliff. He and Catherine became close friends but Hindley was jealous of his father's love for Heathcliff.

When Mr Earnshaw died and Hindley, married by then, became master of Wuthering Heights he degraded Heathcliff into becoming an uncouth servant and encouraged Catherine's friendship with the effete Edgar Linton, the son of the family at Thrushcross Grange. Hindley's wife died soon after giving birth to their son, Hareton, and Hindley became savage with drink and misery. Edgar Linton asked Catherine to marry him; Heathcliff overheard her discussing it with Ellen, saying that though she loved Heathcliff it would demean her to marry him, and he crept away and disappeared. Catherine went out in the rain to search for him and became seriously ill as a result of getting soaked; three years after her recovery she married Edgar, whose parents were dead by then, and went with Ellen to live at the Grange.

She and Edgar were happy until Heathcliff reappeared, transformed into a wealthy and educated man. Edgar was jealous of Catherine's affection for him and Ellen wondered why he was living at the Heights where he gambled with Hindley and encouraged little Hareton in his barbaric behaviour. Isabella, Edgar's sister, became infatuated with Heathcliff who encouraged her; after an angry scene between Edgar and Heathcliff, Catherine became hysterical and locked herself in her room. She remained there for three days, and when Ellen was allowed in she was delirious and imagining herself at the Heights. Though she was feverish she leant out of the window into the icy wind, saying that the only way she could get back to the Heights and be reunited with

Heathcliff was through death. She fell desperately ill; Edgar was so concerned about her he did not try to bring back his sister when she eloped with Heathcliff.

Catherine recovered but remained frail, partly because she was pregnant; after two months Heathcliff and Isabella returned to the Heights. Isabella wrote to Ellen saying what a desolate place it was; Ellen visited her there and saw that Heathcliff hated Isabella and loved only Catherine. She arranged a meeting between Heathcliff and Catherine, and they wept and embraced each other; they were interrupted by Edgar and Catherine lost consciousness. She died after she had given birth to a daughter, Cathy. Heathcliff was violent in his grief. Isabella appeared at the Grange on the night after Catherine's funeral, dishevelled and bleeding from a wound in her neck. She told Ellen how Heathcliff and Hindley had had a brutal fight, and how she had so enraged Heathcliff that he had thrown a knife at her. She threw it back and escaped, and left the Grange to live near London where she bore a son, Linton. Six months after Catherine's death Hindley died; there was some mystery about his death as his servant Joseph implied that Heathcliff murdered him. All Hindley's lands and property became Heathcliff's because of Hindley's gambling debts to him.

In the following twelve years Cathy Linton grew up, cared for by Ellen; then Isabella died and Linton Heathcliff was brought to the Grange but claimed by Heathcliff the same night and taken to the Heights next day; he was a sickly, effeminate boy. Cathy was not allowed to go to the Heights but tricked Ellen into taking her when she was sixteen. Heathcliff told Ellen he wanted the cousins to marry, with the implication that he hoped to inherit the Grange as Linton was clearly frail; Linton would inherit the Grange after Edgar but after his death the property would pass to Cathy. Edgar forbade Cathy to go to the Heights again but she began secretly exchanging love-letters with Linton. Ellen put a stop to that but eventually Heathcliff persuaded Cathy to visit Linton at the Heights, though she did so reluctantly as her father had become very ill. During an illness of Ellen's, Cathy visited the Heights frequently in secret; in response to a letter from Linton, Edgar allowed Cathy to meet Linton twice on the moors but she and Ellen were tricked into entering the Heights the second time.

Here Ellen was kept prisoner for five days while Cathy was forced to marry Linton. Soon after Ellen's return to the Grange, Cathy escaped and followed her, in time to be with her father when he died. Heathcliff claimed the Grange and all Edgar's property; he rented the Grange to Lockwood and took Cathy to live at the Heights. She was left alone to care for Linton, who died soon after she arrived; Hareton tried clumsily to befriend her but she became bitter and scornful of him.

Ellen Dean's story ends here, and Lockwood visits the Heights again to say that he is leaving the neighbourhood; he sees Cathy tormenting Hareton about his inability to read. He returns to the Grange in the autumn of 1802 and again visits the Heights where he sees Cathy and Hareton, who have now become lovers. Ellen Dean is there and Heathcliff dead, so he asks her for an explanation. She tells him that Heathcliff transferred her to the Grange soon after Lockwood's departure and describes how Cathy and Hareton fell in love. At the same time Heathcliff's desire for revenge on Hindley and Edgar and their families seemed to weaken; he told Ellen that he saw Catherine everywhere, and began to go without food. Ellen found him dead one morning beside the window where Lockwood had had his dream. Ellen mentions that villagers say they have seen the ghosts of Heathcliff and Catherine in and around the Heights. Lockwood goes home, passing the graves of Edgar and Heathcliff with Catherine's between them.

Detailed summaries

Volume I Chapter 1

Mr Lockwood, the new tenant of Thrushcross Grange in Yorkshire, begins his diary in 1801 with an account of his first visit to Wuthering Heights, the home of his landlord, Heathcliff. He is not made welcome by either Heathcliff or his servant, Joseph. The grounds are neglected; the house is in an exposed position but it has been ornately built, with the date of its construction, 1500, and the name Hareton Earnshaw carved over the door. Heathcliff strikes Lockwood as incongruous in this setting as he seems more a gentleman than a prosperous but unsophisticated farmer.

After a digression about his own folly in a relationship with a young woman Lockwood describes how Heathcliff leaves him alone with a room full of savage dogs; he grimaces at them and they attack him. The housekeeper rescues him but Heathcliff is amused and becomes more hospitable, which prompts Lockwood to promise to return the next day.

NOTES AND GLOSSARY:
The contrast in dialogue between Heathcliff and Lockwood indicates that Lockwood is an over-sophisticated man of leisure; words like 'penetralium' were not in common currency. Heathcliff's 'Walk in!' is almost rude. The term 'gentleman' as Lockwood uses it relates to Heathcliff's bearing and education. A farmer might be wealthy but would not be classified as a gentleman if his manner lacked refinement.

never . . .underdrawn: the rafters of the roof showed because no ceiling had been constructed under it. This seems primitive to Lockwood

'never told my love': Lockwood is quoting from Shakespeare's *Twelfth Night* (II.iv.109)

Volume I Chapter 2

The following afternoon Lockwood walks to the Heights, arriving as a snow storm begins. No one lets him in until a young man returning from work leads him in through the yard. A pretty but unfriendly young woman whom Lockwood assumes to be Heathcliff's wife is in the living room; Lockwood fails to ingratiate himself with her. Heathcliff comes in, startling Lockwood by the savage tone he uses to the woman. At tea, Lockwood tries to make conversation but only antagonises the young man, Hareton Earnshaw, by trying to guess the relationships in the family. Heathcliff explains briefly that both his wife and his son are dead, and that the young woman is the widow of his dead son; he seems to Lockwood to hate her.

Meanwhile snow falls thickly. Lockwood wants to go home but no one takes any notice of him; Mrs Heathcliff and Joseph, the servant, bicker. Heathcliff insults Lockwood and he snatches Joseph's lantern and tries to get away. Two dogs knock him down, his nose bleeds violently, and Zillah, the housekeeper, comes to his aid and shows him to a bedroom for the night.

NOTES AND GLOSSARY:
Lockwood's reference to his dinner hour highlights the contrast between the social sphere to which he belongs and that into which he has come. In polite southern society the dinner hour was five; in the north, particularly in the country and in the lower social classes, dinner was served much earlier.

'threats . . .smacked of King Lear': for example, 'I will have such revenges on you both', Shakespeare, *King Lear*, II.iv.282
'Whet are ye for? . . .: Joseph speaks a broad Yorkshire dialect. His speeches from 'Whet are ye for?' to 'hend wi't' mean: 'What do you want?' 'The master's down in the sheepfold. Go round by the end of the barn if you want to speak to him,' 'There's no one but the mistress; and she'll not open it if you go on making your fearful din until night.' 'Not I! I'll have nothing to do with it.'
'Aw woonder . . .afore ye!': 'I wonder how you have the face to stand there in idleness and worse, when they've all gone out. But you're useless, and it's no use talking – you'll never mend your evil ways; but go straight to the devil like your mother before you.'

discussed:	consumed
agait:	afoot

Volume I Chapter 3

Lockwood climbs into the box-bed (a bed enclosed by panelling) in his room and finds a name scratched on the window-sill within, and some old books which have been scribbled on by the child they belonged to twenty-five years earlier. He reads her account of a wet Sunday when she and Heathcliff had to listen to a sermon from Joseph in a cold attic while her brother and his wife enjoyed themselves by the fire. When they protested they were thrown into the back kitchen. She took up the story later saying that she and Heathcliff had been punished, presumably for escaping for a scamper on the moors. Lockwood becomes drowsy and has a dream that he is going through the snow with Joseph to hear an interminable sermon in a chapel; the dream ends as he fights the congregation and the preacher bangs the pulpit. He wakes to find a branch tapping on the window beside him, and dozes again, dreaming that he breaks the window to get hold of the branch and his hand is grasped by icy fingers, while a voice begs to be let in. He sees a child's face at the window and gashes its wrist in an attempt to make the hand let go of him; still the voice moans that it has been a waif for twenty years. Lockwood shouts with fright and Heathcliff appears, over-wrought and irritable. When Lockwood has described his dream to him, and Heathcliff thinks he has gone, he hears Heathcliff open the window and plead with Catherine to return. Lockwood passes the rest of the night in the kitchen and is escorted back to Thrushcross Grange by Heathcliff.

NOTES AND GLOSSARY:

'T'maister . . .sowls!': Joseph has superstition and Christianity inextricably confused. 'The master's only just buried, and Sunday not over and the sound of the Gospel still in your ears and you dare be playing! shame on you! sit down, wicked children! there are enough good books if you'll read them; sit down and think of your souls!'

'Maister . . .goan!': 'Master, come here! Miss Cathy's torn the back off *The Helmet of Salvation* and Heathcliff has kicked his feet into the first part of *The Broad Way to Destruction*! It's awful of you to let them carry on in this way. Ah, the old man would have beaten them properly – but he's gone!'

the sin that no Christian need pardon: blasphemy against the Holy Ghost is the unforgivable sin, the Bible, Luke 12:10

Why did I think of *'Linton'* . . .: Emily Brontë draws the reader's attention to the three names, Linton, Earnshaw and Heathcliff, through Lockwood's dream.
'that the place . . .no more!': from the Bible, Job 7:10
'Thou art the Man!': from the Bible, II Samuel 12:7
'the judgment written!': Psalm 149:9
lean type:	bad type
scroop:	spine, back
ideal:	imaginary
Grimalkin:	name for a cat
sotto voce:	under his breath

Volume I Chapter 4

Lockwood feels ill so he asks his housekeeper to sit with him. She tells him that the woman at the Heights was her dead master's daughter, formerly Catherine Linton, cousin both to her dead husband and to Hareton Earnshaw. Mrs Dean was nurse to Catherine and Lockwood leads her into telling Heathcliff's story. As a child, she was companion to Hindley, Hareton's father, and his sister Catherine, and describes the day when their father walked home from Liverpool bringing with him a destitute child he had found in the streets there. The boy was dirty, swarthy, and his speech was unintelligible. Though no one welcomed him at first, Catherine, who was about his age, became his close friend after a few days. Hindley hated the boy, now named Heathcliff, and he and Ellen Dean treated him spitefully; Ellen changed her attitude to him when she nursed him through measles. Mr Earnshaw made a favourite of Heathcliff, which Hindley resented. Ellen gives an example of Heathcliff's knowledge of his power over Mr Earnshaw and of his ability to endure pain, and of Hindley's vindictiveness.

NOTES AND GLOSSARY: .
The double narrative begins in this chapter and continues for most of the novel, with Lockwood telling the reader what Mrs Dean told him.

Mrs Dean:	Mrs was used as a courtesy title; Ellen was not married
Liverpool:	a large seaport where there would have been many abandoned children on the streets in 1771
the cuckoo and the dunnock:	the cuckoo lays its one egg in another bird's nest. The fledgling cuckoo gradually pushes out all the eggs or fledglings in the nest and then has the parent birds' attention for itself. A dunnock is a hedge-sparrow; Hareton is being compared to the helpless fledgling pushed from the nest

strike my colours: military metaphor meaning he surrendered
indigenae: local people

Volume 1 Chapter 5

Ellen tells how Mr Earnshaw weakened, and became particularly irritable with Hindley, while Joseph tormented him with tales of the children's mischief. Catherine was high-spirited, wayward, and captivating. She and Heathcliff were constant companions; Heathcliff's devotion to her was painful to Mr Earnshaw, to whom Heathcliff showed little affection. One October night when Hindley had been sent away to college, Catherine sang her father to sleep, to compensate for having offended him. He died in his sleep, causing Heathcliff and Catherine great grief. Later when Ellen looked into the bedroom they shared she overheard them comforting each other by imagining what heaven would be like.

NOTES AND GLOSSARY:
wick: lively
frame: go quickly

Volume I Chapter 6

When Hindley returned for his father's funeral he brought a wife, Frances, who was frightened by the funeral and showed ominous nervous symptoms to which Ellen was unsympathetic. Hindley would not allow Heathcliff, Catherine or the servants into the living room; Heathcliff was degraded to a farm labourer and he and Catherine became wilder and careless of incurring punishment. One night when they did not return from the moors Hindley locked the house against them; Ellen waited up and met Heathcliff as he came home alone. He told her that they had peered through the windows of Thrushcross Grange and seen the spoilt Linton children squabbling over a lapdog. They laughed and the Lintons heard them and set dogs on them. A bull-dog caught Catherine's ankle; she fainted and a servant carried her into the house where she was recognised by Edgar Linton. Heathcliff was sent home but waited outside the window to see that Catherine was well cared for; he thought her superior to everyone. As a result of a visit to Hindley from Mr Linton complaining of the children's behaviour Heathcliff was forbidden to speak to Catherine again.

NOTES AND GLOSSARY:
The chronology of the novel is complex; the narrative in this chapter takes us back to Catherine's diary, read by Lockwood in Chapter 3. Frances's symptoms suggest that she has tuberculosis of the lung, a

disease which was a major cause of death in nineteenth-century Britain; Emily Brontë herself and three of her sisters died of it.

'you shall go to the gallows': hanging was at that time the punishment for insignificant offences against property
foreigners: strangers
delf-case: a cupboard for crockery. Delft ware was glazed pottery made in Holland and later popularised and copied in England
basement: ledge above the level of the basement
out-and-outer: slang term for rascal
negus: hot wine and water

Volume I Chapter 7

Catherine returned from the Grange at Christmas, her unfeminine behaviour transformed into that of a young lady. Heathcliff had become more filthy and unkempt, and Catherine laughed at his sullenness as she greeted him. This made him run away and refuse to come into the kitchen to be washed although it was Christmas Eve. The following morning he changed his mind and allowed Ellen to wash him and coax him into a good temper. He showed his jealousy of Edgar Linton but Ellen tried to persuade him that he was more handsome and manly than Linton. Heathcliff went out to greet Catherine, who had come back from church with the Linton children as her guests, but Hindley prevented him. Then Edgar irritated Heathcliff so he emptied hot sauce over him. Hindley beat Heathcliff and locked him in an attic; Catherine seemed unmoved but could not eat and escaped in the evening to join Heathcliff. He consoled himself by planning his revenge on Hindley. Here Mrs Dean breaks off but Lockwood begs her to stay and continue her story though it is eleven at night; he feels that life in the country is lived at a more intense level than it is in the town. He comments on Mrs Dean's thoughtful and intelligent manner which he finds surprising in a servant; she replies that she has been made to think and has read most of the books in the library.

NOTES AND GLOSSARY:
beaver: hat made of beaver fur
habit: riding costume
cant: brisk
donning: dressing
coxcomb: vain and foolish man
cambric: fine linen
mess of victuals: portion of food
long hours: hours before midnight

Volume I Chapter 8

Mrs Dean's narrative now passes on to the summer of 1778 when Hareton Earnshaw was born and his mother, Frances, died of tuberculosis. Hindley became savage and dissipated after her death, driving all the servants but Joseph and Ellen away and ill-treating Heathcliff. Catherine became the most attractive girl in the neighbourhood and Edgar Linton was in love with her, though he rarely visited the Heights as he feared Hindley. Heathcliff was so brutalised that he had become repulsive, though Catherine still spent much of her time with him. One day when Hindley was away she had asked Edgar to call and Heathcliff decided to stay at home too. Irritated by this, she complained that he was dull company and drove him out of the house as Edgar arrived. Ellen annoyed Catherine who pinched and slapped her, shook the baby Hareton, and hit Edgar when he tried to intervene. Edgar attempted to leave, in astonished outrage, but Catherine stopped him by beginning to weep and they emerged from the quarrel as lovers.

NOTES AND GLOSSARY:
rush of a lass: a frail girl
marred: spoilt
lime: used to make barren soil more fertile

Volume I Chapter 9

Hindley came home violently drunk and dropped little Hareton over the banisters but Heathcliff caught him, regretting the action afterwards. Ellen settled in the kitchen thinking she was alone but Heathcliff was hidden in a corner. Catherine came in and told Ellen that she wanted advice as she had just agreed to marry Edgar. Her reasons for loving him were for his looks, youth and wealth; she said she was only concerned with the present, and yet she was uneasy. She explained through recounting a dream that she could not marry Heathcliff as he had been so degraded by Hindley (here Heathcliff crept out of the room) but she felt that her soul and Heathcliff's were the same and Edgar's was quite different. She claimed that she would be able to help Heathcliff with Edgar's money and had no intention of being separated from him after her marriage as she felt he was part of her being. Joseph returned but Heathcliff did not. Ellen told Catherine that Heathcliff had overheard her. Catherine got soaked with rain during a storm when she went out to look for Heathcliff. At midnight the storm split a tree that knocked a chimney over. Catherine sat up all night in her wet clothes and was feverish by morning. Heathcliff did not reappear and Catherine became ill with brain fever; both Mr and Mrs Linton caught it and died.

Three years later Catherine married Edgar and she and Ellen went to the Grange to live. Here Ellen stops her story as it is half past one in the morning and Lockwood, feeling ill, goes to bed.

NOTES AND GLOSSARY:

It was far in the night . . .: Ellen's song is from 'The Ghost's Warning', a ballad

bairnies: children

grat: wept

mither: mother

beneath the mools: under the earth

fate of Milo: he was eaten by wild animals when he tried to pull up a tree which held him by his hands

the patriarchs Noah and Lot. in the Bible Noah and Lot were spared by God when he destroyed the wicked. Jonah had to be put over the side of a ship during a storm to save the other passengers

All works . . . rubbidge: from the Bible, the Book of Romans 8:28

girt eedle seeght: great idle sight

fahl: foul

war un' war: worse and worse

rigs: ridges

plottered: blundered

offald: worthless

Aw sud more likker: I should more likely

Aw's niver wonder: I shouldn't wonder

starving: frozen

bog-hoile: hole in the marsh

gentle and simple: of all classes

yon cat uh Linton: that cat of a Linton

wer: our

uf hor side: for her part

th'hahs: the house

Volume I Chapter 10

Lockwood resumes his diary after four weeks' illness and calls Mrs Dean to continue her story. She recounts that Edgar and Catherine were very happy until Heathcliff appeared at the Grange looking intelligent, dignified, and retaining nothing of his former degradation. Catherine's rapture when she saw him irritated Edgar. Ellen wondered why Heathcliff was staying with Hindley at the Heights, but Catherine explained that Hindley wanted him there to gamble with him. Catherine appeased Edgar but his sister, Isabella, imagined herself in love with

Heathcliff. He had no interest in her feelings, only in her property. Ellen reported to Isabella that Hindley was badly in debt to Heathcliff but she persisted in idolising him.

NOTES AND GLOSSARY:

sizer:	an undergraduate at Cambridge who received financial help from his college
America:	the War of American Independence, 1776–83
Coroner's inquest:	an inquiry held into a death not apparently attributable to natural causes
grand 'sizes:	the Grand Assizes; here, judgement after death
Broad road:	that leads to destruction (from the Bible, Matthew 7:13)
centipede from the Indies:	the West Indian centipede is venomous
phalanx of vials:	rows of bottles
sough:	ditch
beck:	stream
jubilee:	occasion for celebration
we's hae . . . folks:	we shall have a Coroner's inquest at our house soon
wi' hauding . . . cawlf:	as a result of stopping the other from killing himself as a calf is killed
ut's . . . going:	who so wants to go
banning:	swearing
girn a laugh:	snarl a laugh
lugs:	ears
wah . . . brass:	why, he can count his money
t'pikes:	the gates
dog in the manger:	selfish person

Volume I Chapter 11

Ellen comments to Lockwood that she had often set off to speak to her old playmate, Hindley, about what was happening to him, but turned back; once she reached the Heights and saw Hareton who swore at her and expressed his fondness for Heathcliff. She ran away when she saw Heathcliff. He continued to visit the Grange and was seen embracing Isabella by Ellen. She shouted a protest which Catherine heard, and a quarrel took place between Catherine and Heathcliff. He claimed that she had treated him cruelly; she pretended not to understand, and became agitated. Ellen asked Edgar to intervene, and in the scene that followed Heathcliff was abusive to Edgar, Edgar hit him and went to fetch servants to help him turn Heathcliff out. Heathcliff escaped and Catherine became hysterical with Edgar, having decided to break Edgar's and Heathcliff's hearts by breaking her own if she could not get what she wanted in any other way. She ran up to her bedroom and locked herself in, refusing food and drink for two days. Edgar warned Isabella that he would have nothing more to do with her if she encouraged Heathcliff as a suitor.

NOTES AND GLOSSARY:
sand pillar: a milestone
barn: bairn, child

Volume I Chapter 12

On the third day Catherine opened her door to ask for water and food as she thought she was dying; Ellen remained unsympathetic, though Catherine looked ill. Catherine was frightened of dying in the Grange and kept asking Ellen to open the window; she became delirious and imagined she was a child on the moors with Heathcliff, then that she was in the room she used to share with Heathcliff at the Heights. She longed to be a girl again out on the moors and opened the window so that the icy wind blew round her; leaning out she imagined that she could see the lights in Wuthering Heights and dared Heathcliff to follow her into the grave. She said she would never rest in the grave until he was with her. Edgar came in and was horrified to see how ill Catherine was; she said she no longer needed him and would be dead by the spring. Both Edgar and Catherine blamed Ellen for what had happened; she ran for the doctor, stopping on the way to rescue Isabella's dog which was hanging from a hook in the wall. As Ellen returned with the doctor she guessed from his gossip that Isabella had run away with Heathcliff and returned home to find her room empty. When Edgar discovered what had happened he said that his sister had disowned him and ordered Ellen to send her belongings to her new home, when she knew where it was to be.

NOTES AND GLOSSARY:
pigeon's feathers: there was a superstition that the soul of a dying person could not leave the body if it lay on a bed containing pigeon feathers
fairy cave: all caves were believed to be inhabited by fairies
elf-bolts: a flint arrowhead, believed to be shot by fairies at cattle
springer: a kind of spaniel
caps them: outdoes them

Volume I Chapter 13

In the two months that Heathcliff and Isabella were away Catherine's brain-fever abated and she recovered, though she remained frail and depressed. Here Ellen reads Lockwood a letter she received from

Isabella on her return to the Heights with Heathcliff. She described how Hareton swore at her, Joseph mocked her, and Heathcliff left her alone on their arrival. Hindley showed her a weapon and expressed his fear that he would kill Heathcliff before he had won his own money and Heathcliff's from him. Isabella tried to make the porridge for supper but did it badly; she then searched the house for a bedroom, as Heathcliff's was locked. In desperation she threw her supper tray on the ground and wept; eventually she had the filthy living room to herself when Joseph, Hindley and Hareton went to bed. She fell asleep, to be roused by Heathcliff's violent abuse. The letter ended with her acknowledgement of her hatred of Heathcliff and hope that Ellen would visit her.

NOTES AND GLOSSARY:

dip-candle:	candle made by dipping wick in melted tallow
lantern jaws:	long thin jaws giving a hollow appearance to the face
cut paper:	pictures cut from coloured paper and pasted on, probably done by Hindley's dead wife, Frances
valances:	drapery hanging round the canopy of a bed
elder:	lay officer in Presbyterian churches
mim:	prim, affected
minching and munching:	mocking abuse of Isabella's voice
If they's . . . ortherings:	if there are to be new arrangements
flitting:	moving
Aw daht:	I'm afraid
thible:	wooden spoon
maw nave:	my fist
pale t'guilp off:	skim the froth off
deaved aht:	knocked out
cranky:	shaky
meeterly:	tolerably
baht all this wark:	without all this trouble
mells on't:	interferes with it
madling:	fool
They's . . . dahn in:	there's not another room to lie down in
plisky:	tantrum
pining:	starving
Him as allas makes a third:	the Devil

Volume I Chapter 14

When she received the letter Ellen went to Edgar, asking him to write a note of forgiveness which she would take to Isabella, but he refused. Ellen went to the Heights and found Isabella looking slovenly and the house dreary; only Heathcliff looked presentable. Isabella was disappointed to receive nothing from Edgar. Heathcliff began to insist that he must see Catherine; Ellen tried to dissuade him, saying that more emotional turmoil would endanger Catherine's life. Heathcliff asserted that the love between him and Catherine was stronger than anything between Catherine and Edgar; he abused Isabella for her self-delusion in marrying him. He sent her upstairs and persuaded Ellen to arrange a meeting between him and Catherine. Lockwood comments on the dullness of Ellen Dean's story and the lesson it has taught him, that he must avoid the attractions of Catherine Heathcliff.

NOTES AND GLOSSARY:

brach:	bitch-hound
dree:	cheerless
taking:	plight

Volume II Chapter 1

(*In many editions of the book the chapters are numbered straight through from one to thirty-four, ignoring the original division into two volumes.*)

Lockwood takes up his journal a week later having heard Ellen's whole story. She gave Catherine a note from Heathcliff one warm Sunday evening in spring when Edgar was at church. Although Catherine was apparently recovering from her illness her abstraction and pallor convinced Ellen that she must soon die. She could not read the letter, but Heathcliff himself entered immediately and clasped her in his arms. Catherine claimed that he and Edgar had killed her between them and would forget her soon after her death; Heathcliff replied that he could as soon forget himself as her. Catherine, after expressing her longing to escape from her ruined body, appealed to Heathcliff to come to her, and he caught her close to him, refusing to allow Ellen near her. He reproached her for her betrayal of him and of her own heart, and she replied that she was dying for her mistake. As they wept and kissed each other Ellen began to worry about Edgar's return. She saw him coming and Heathcliff tried to leave but Catherine clung to him shrieking that she would die if he went. Edgar came in to find Catherine unconscious in Heathcliff's arms. Edgar and Ellen tried to restore Catherine to consciousness while Heathcliff waited outside in the garden.

Volume II Chapter 2

At midnight that night Catherine died after giving birth to a premature daughter, not the male heir that had been hoped for. Ellen speculates about whether Catherine's soul can be at peace, then goes on to describe how she found Heathcliff beside himself with grief in the grounds of the Grange, praying to Catherine's spirit to haunt him and dashing his head against a tree. Catherine's body lay in the house for several days; one night Heathcliff came in and removed a curl of Edgar's hair from a locket round the corpse's neck, and replaced it with his own hair. Ellen twisted the two together and put them into the locket. Catherine was buried outside the chapel in a corner of the churchyard, where her husband is now buried with her.

NOTES AND GLOSSARY:
For the sake of clarity the older Catherine will be referred to as Catherine and her daughter as Cathy.

his being left without an heir: it seems clear that old Mr Linton left his estate to Edgar and his sons, but that Edgar's daughters were passed over in favour of his sister and her sons. So Heathcliff's wife will inherit the Grange if Edgar does not remarry and have sons

---

Volume II Chapter 3

The day after Catherine's funeral the weather became wintry again and Ellen was sitting nursing the baby when Isabella, dishevelled, cold, and bleeding from a wound in her neck, burst into the room. After she had changed her clothes and smashed her wedding ring because it was Heathcliff's she sat with Ellen and told her what had happened. She was determined to leave the area as Heathcliff would not let her remain at the Grange. The previous day she had been sitting with Hindley when Heathcliff, who had kept away from her in his grief over Catherine's death, arrived home. The door was locked, and Hindley locked the front door too, then asked Isabella if she would sit silent while he murdered Heathcliff. Isabella shouted a warning to Heathcliff through the window then sat down again. Heathcliff broke a window open and grasped Hindley's weapon through it; it gashed Hindley's wrist so badly that he fainted, and Heathcliff, breaking in through the window, kicked him and beat his head on the floor. Joseph was called to attend to Hindley and wanted to go for Edgar Linton, the magistrate, but Heathcliff forced Isabella to describe what had happened. The following day both Hindley and Heathcliff looked pale and thin; Isabella taunted Heathcliff about Catherine's death and he threw a knife at her, hitting her below her ear. She threw it back and ran away as Hindley and Heathcliff began to fight.

Having told her story she left for the south of England where she gave birth to a frail son, Linton. Heathcliff knew of her whereabouts and of the child. Edgar grew to love his daughter. Six months after her birth

Hindley died after a night's drinking. Joseph tells Ellen that when he left Hindley with Heathcliff he was far from dead but when he returned with the doctor he was. Ellen attended Hindley's funeral; Heathcliff became owner of the Heights and threatened that if Edgar took Hareton from him he would take Linton from Isabella, so Edgar did not interfere, and Hareton lived on at the Heights like a servant.

NOTES AND GLOSSARY:

nip up the corner of your apron: to dry her tears
the fool's body should be buried at the cross-roads: normally the punishment for criminals who committed suicide while awaiting execution
so as by fire: from the Bible, 1 Corinthians 3:15
an eye for an eye, tooth for a tooth: from the Bible, Exodus 21:24
girned: snarled
flags: flagstone floor
stark: rigid
taen tent: taken care

Volume II Chapter 4

Mrs Dean described the next twelve years as the happiest in her life. Cathy grew up beautiful and affectionate; her father never allowed her out of the park round the Grange. When she was twelve her aunt Isabella became seriously ill; Edgar went to visit her immediately and Cathy tricked Ellen into thinking that she was spending the day in the park when she was in fact riding her pony up to the Heights. Ellen went in search of her and found her there. Cathy misunderstood Hareton's position and took him for a servant; the servant at the Heights reproved her for speaking rudely to her cousin. This disturbed her and she cried that her father had gone to fetch her real cousin. Ellen was alarmed, knowing that this would be repeated to Heathcliff when he came back. Ellen took Cathy home after Hareton had brought her pony; he was tall, handsome and not unkind, though Heathcliff had made him as brutal as he could, and Hareton could not read or write.

NOTES AND GLOSSARY:

pointers: kind of hound used to scent game
galloway: small riding horse
Mr Heathcliff's place: 'place' is used here in the old sense of a country house with grounds
wicket: gate
fairishes: fairies
wisht: be quiet
offalld: awful

Volume II Chapter 5

Isabella died and Edgar returned home with Linton, his nephew. Cathy longed for them to arrive but when they did Linton, who was pale and sickly, wept and complained. Ellen got him to sleep but Joseph arrived immediately demanding that he should take Linton back to the Heights with him. Edgar refused this but promised that he should go the next day, though Isabella had hoped that Edgar could keep him.

NOTES AND GLOSSARY:

unlikely: unsuitable
donned in: dressed in
Hathecliff . . . norther: Heathcliff takes no account of the mother, or of you, either
he's come: he will come

Volume II Chapter 6

The following morning Ellen took Linton to the Heights before breakfast. He had never heard of his father and was reluctant to go. When they arrived Heathcliff laughed scornfully at his fair skin and frailty. He promised Ellen he would take care of him as he wanted him to inherit the Grange and become master over the Lintons. Linton refused to eat the food he was offered and cried as Ellen left him.

NOTES AND GLOSSARY:

brown study: deep thought
ague: fever, or fit of shaking
cipher: nonentity

Volume II Chapter 7

Cathy was disappointed that Linton had gone the next morning; she was not told where he was though Ellen heard that Linton had become petulant and selfish living at the Heights. Cathy did not see Linton again until her sixteenth birthday, when she tricked Ellen again, this time into walking with her close to the Heights. They met Heathcliff who persuaded Cathy to visit the Heights, though Ellen was reluctant to do so; Heathcliff told her he wanted the two cousins to fall in love and marry. There Cathy found Linton, to her delight, and also discovered that Heathcliff and her father had quarrelled. Heathcliff muttered to Ellen that he wished Hareton had been his son instead of the feeble Linton who wanted to stay by the fire instead of walking with Cathy. Hareton, having washed, was persuaded to take Cathy for a walk round the farm. Heathcliff confided to Ellen that he had had his revenge on

Hindley by degrading Hareton and at the same time making Hareton fond of him. Linton went out to join Cathy, and they laughed at Hareton's inability to read. The following morning Cathy accused her father of preventing her from being friends with Linton; Edgar explained his reasons briefly but in the evening Ellen found Cathy weeping because she had promised to see Linton the next day and her father forbade it. She tried to write Linton a note but Ellen stopped her; several weeks later however Ellen discovered that Cathy was using the milk boy to send love letters to Linton and to receive them from him. Some of those from Linton seemed to Ellen to have been partly written by Heathcliff; she burnt them all in Cathy's presence, threatening that if Cathy kept any Ellen would tell Edgar about them. She sent a message to Linton asking him to send no more notes.

NOTES AND GLOSSARY:

pinched:	cold or hungry
slop:	contemptuous term for invalid's food
mummy:	a pulpy substance
moor game:	grouse
nab:	a jutting-out part of hill or rock
gaumless:	foolish
bathos:	depth
faster:	more firmly
extra-animal:	not animal
lath:	weakling
the stand of hives:	structure on which hives are placed

Volume II Chapter 8

That autumn Edgar became ill and had to stay indoors; Ellen kept Cathy company in a walk in the park and assured her that her father would recover if Cathy did not worry him by showing her feeling for Linton. Cathy said she loved no one as much as her father. She climbed up a wall by a locked gate into the park. Her hat fell down outside, she climbed after it and could not get up again. While Ellen was trying to unlock the gate Heathcliff rode past; he persuaded Cathy that Linton was dying for love of her and begged her to visit the Heights. Cathy was so disturbed that Ellen set off with her to the Heights the following day.

NOTES AND GLOSSARY:

diurnal:	daily
starved and sackless:	frozen and dispirited
canty:	cheerful
stretched:	made our way quickly
Slough of Despond:	a reference to John Bunyan's *The Pilgrim's Progress*

Volume II Chapter 9

It was a cold wet day; when they reached the Heights Linton was alone and whining. Cathy and Linton argued about whether their fathers and mothers loved each other and Cathy pushed his chair which caused him a prolonged fit of coughing. She was so frightened by his moaning that she stayed all the morning trying to comfort him; eventually she coaxed him into a better temper though Ellen regarded him as being too tiresome to bother with. On the way home Ellen said it would be a relief for his family if Linton died young, as she thought likely. Cathy became upset, but Ellen warned her that she must not see Linton again. As a result of getting wet Ellen was ill for three weeks; Cathy nursed her but visited Linton secretly every evening.

NOTES AND GLOSSARY:

elysium:	heaven
win:	reach
drops off:	dies
gadding off:	wandering off to enjoy oneself
laid up:	ill in bed

Volume II Chapter 10

When Ellen was up again she could not understand why Cathy made excuses to leave her every evening until she caught her coming back from a ride to the Heights. Cathy told her that the first time she went she and Linton had a happy evening but the next night Hareton was waiting for her. He wanted to show her that he could read his name, carved over the door, but Cathy laughed at him and as a result he turned her and Linton out of the living room. Linton's ugly rage made him cough blood; Cathy wept and ran for Zillah, the housekeeper, to help. Hareton tried to apologise as she rode home but she cut him with her whip. The next time she went Linton blamed her for the upheaval and she left immediately. Two nights later she returned out of a sense of duty and Linton asked her to forgive him; she told Ellen she had learnt to tolerate his perversity. Ellen went straight to Edgar and told him the whole story, and Edgar said that Cathy was not to visit the Heights again.

NOTES AND GLOSSARY:

overdone:	overcome
casement window:	glass doors
frame:	invent
throstles:	thrushes
conned:	learned
sarve ye aht:	get his own back on you

skift:	shift
orther:	either
what was there to do?:	what was the matter?
no sich stuff:	no such thing
bahn:	going
blubbering:	crying (*contemptuous*)

Volume II Chapter 11

Ellen tells Lockwood that all this happened a year ago; she wonders if he will fall in love with Cathy himself, though he says he wishes to return to the busy world. Ellen goes on to describe Edgar's anxiety as he felt his death approaching, and Cathy's obedience to him. He wrote to Linton inviting him to the Grange; Linton wrote in reply asking to be allowed to meet his cousin. Eventually Edgar agreed that they should walk or ride together on the moors once a week as he wanted them to marry to retain the Grange for Cathy. No one knew how ill Linton was or how Heathcliff ill-treated him.

Volume II Chapter 12

Late in the summer Cathy and Ellen set out to meet Linton. They found him lying on the moor near the Heights, too feeble to walk or speak much. Cathy wanted to go home but this frightened Linton and he begged her to stay; he was afraid his father would discover he had been silent and lethargic while he was with her. Cathy thought him stronger because he did not complain; Ellen thought him much worse. Cathy left promising to return the next week.

Volume II Chapter 13

The next week Edgar was clearly dying but Ellen and Cathy made what they intended to be a brief visit to Linton, finding him in the same place. He was terrified that he would be killed if Cathy left him, and intimated that he had a secret of which he was ashamed. Heathcliff arrived asking if Edgar was dying as he was afraid that Linton would die first. Heathcliff bullied Cathy and Ellen into helping Linton to return to the Heights and locked them in as soon as they stepped inside the house. When Cathy tried to seize the key he slapped her. He went away to look for their horses and Linton explained that Heathcliff wanted him to marry Cathy immediately and thought Edgar would object. Heathcliff returned and made clear that if Cathy would not marry Linton she should remain a prisoner until Edgar died, and that it would delight him to make Edgar miserable. Three servants came from the Grange to look for Cathy but Heathcliff headed them off and locked Cathy and Ellen in a garret. The next morning Heathcliff came and took Cathy away but Ellen had to stay for five nights with Hareton as her jailer.

NOTES AND GLOSSARY:

without benefit of clergy: Ellen seems to mean that only a clergyman can legally marry Cathy and Linton

changeling: a child surreptitiously put in exchange for another, associated in folklore with fairy children being substituted for human babies

bespeak: beg for

hearth-stone: fireside

ling: heather

Lees: grazing ground for cattle

spleen: bad temper

cockatrice: mythical poisonous snake-like creature

eft: a small lizard

chit: girl (*contemptuous*)

Volume II Chapter 14

Zillah let Ellen out, telling her the rumours about her disappearance current in Gimmerton. Linton was downstairs and told Ellen he was married to Cathy and all her possessions were now his, though she was weeping constantly for her father. She had tried to bribe Linton to release her with a locket containing portraits of her father and mother. Heathcliff had come in and taken Catherine's portrait and crushed Edgar's. Linton refused to release Cathy so Ellen hurried home to find Edgar close to death. He asked for Cathy and Ellen sent servants to the Heights to rescue her and a man to fetch the attorney as Edgar wished to alter his will, to put Cathy's fortune in the hands of trustees and so to protect it from Heathcliff. The attorney had been bribed by Heathcliff to ignore a summons from Edgar, and the servants who went to fetch Cathy returned without her but during the night Cathy returned, having escaped from the Heights with Linton's help, and was with her father when he died. The attorney dismissed all the servants and tried to prevent Edgar from being buried beside Catherine but Ellen prevented that.

NOTES AND GLOSSARY:

swung to: hanging from

bespoke: reserved to myself

Volume II Chapter 15

While Ellen and Cathy were sitting in the Grange after Edgar's funeral Heathcliff arrived. He described how he had punished Linton for his part in Cathy's escape and said that she must return with him to the Heights as he was looking for a tenant for the Grange. He refused to allow Ellen to move to the Heights, and ordered that the portrait of Catherine in the Grange should be sent to the Heights next day. Then he told Ellen how he had ordered the sexton, when he was digging Edgar's grave, to clear Catherine's coffin and Heathcliff opened it. He then loosened one side of the coffin and told the sexton to move it and one side of his coffin when he was buried so that his corpse could disintegrate with Catherine's. He dreamt of lying dead beside her in his first peaceful night for eighteen years. He also told Ellen that during the night after Catherine's funeral he had dug up her coffin and was about to open it when he felt someone standing over him and was sure it was Catherine. He refilled the grave and went home accompanied by the mysterious presence and expected to find her in the Heights when he got there, but was disappointed. That experience had been often repeated, exhausting Heathcliff's nerves. Cathy came in and Heathcliff took her to the Heights, warning Ellen that she must not visit her.

NOTES AND GLOSSARY:
cobweb: such a fragile thing
den: hollow
beaten out of that: defeated in that

Volume II Chapter 16

Ellen tells Lockwood that she has tried to visit Cathy but has not been permitted to see her. Zillah had told her that no one at the Heights liked Cathy. When Cathy arrived she found Linton very ill and asked for help; Heathcliff refused to allow anyone to help her and they all left her alone with Linton until he died. Heathcliff showed Cathy Linton's will; he had left all his property and hers to Heathcliff but could not include the land though Heathcliff claimed that. For a fortnight Cathy remained in her room but was so cold that she came downstairs one Sunday afternoon when Heathcliff was out. Hareton smartened himself up and tried to talk to her but when he asked if she would read to him she replied that she had had no kindness when she had needed it and now wanted nothing to do with anyone at the Heights. Hareton protested, then swore at her when she rebuffed him again. This is the end of Ellen's story; Lockwood intends to ride to the Heights soon to tell Heathcliff he is leaving and wants to give up the tenancy of the Grange in October.

NOTES AND GLOSSARY:

the Methodists' or Baptists' place:	Joseph and Zillah are non-conformists. The Kirk would be Church of England
Linton's will:	he was a minor (under twenty-one) when he died and so could not will the lands that he gained by marrying Cathy to his father. Heathcliff however claims a right to them through Isabella and Linton. Cathy could have disputed his possession but would have needed legal help and money to do so
thrang:	busy
moaned hisseln:	moaned to himself
allwildered like:	looking bewildered
fain of:	glad about
a thought bothered:	rather worried
over-looking:	superintendence
train-oil:	whale-oil (for cleaning guns)
happen:	perhaps
doing my little all, that road:	doing what saving I can, in every possible way
in such a taking:	in such a state of rage
stalled of:	bored with
such a concern:	such a creature
curl back:	spring back

Volume II Chapter 17

Lockwood goes to the Heights taking a note from Ellen to Cathy. Heathcliff is out but Lockwood waits with Hareton and Cathy; Cathy taunts Hareton about his attempts to read her books which she says he has stolen. He brings them all and gives them to her and she begins to read from one as he would, whereupon he slaps her and throws the books in the fire. Heathcliff comes in as Hareton leaves, muttering to himself that Hareton looks more and more like Catherine. Lockwood tells him that he is leaving, stays for dinner and goes.

NOTES AND GLOSSARY:

Chevy Chase:	medieval English ballad
causeway:	area paved with cobbles

Volume II Chapter 18

Lockwood resumes his diary later in 1802, recounting his visit to the Grange in September. He finds Ellen has moved to the Heights and nothing is ready for him; while the new housekeeper prepares food and a bed for him he walks up to the Heights. Through the window he sees

Cathy with her arm round Hareton's shoulder teaching him to read; they kiss and wander out on to the moors. Lockwood goes round to the kitchen and finds Ellen sewing and arguing with Joseph. She greets him and gives him the news that Heathcliff is dead; he sits down with a pint of beer to hear about it. She tells him that she was summoned to the Heights a fortnight after he left the Grange and found that Cathy was irritable and fretful. She taunted Hareton constantly but really wanted to be on good terms with him. She tried to interest him in learning to read again but failed until one evening when she, he and Ellen were alone together. Cathy appealed to him to be friendly, and by kissing and coaxing him she persuaded him to look at a book with her. Joseph was horrified to see them together when he returned but they grew dearer to each other.

NOTES AND GLOSSARY:
devastate the moors: go on a shooting expedition
wick: weeks
bluff: steep
bide: live
They's nowt norther dry nor mensful: there's nothing either dry or decent
against my return: ready for my return
Eea, f'r owt Ee knaw: Yes, for all I know
Aw'd rayther, by th'haulf: I'd much rather
nur . . . hahsiver: than have to listen to you, anyway
yah . . . Sattan: you start your pagan singing
fellies: admirers
jocks: food
reaming: frothing, brimful
take a new mind: changing his mind
in following the house: doing the housework
getting up linen: preparing linen
mucky: filthy
Side . . . t'gait: get out of the way
This hoile . . . us: this room is neither decent nor seemly for us
it 'ull be mitch: you'll be lucky

Volume II Chapter 19

The following morning Cathy persuaded Hareton to dig up some of Joseph's bushes to make a garden for her; at breakfast Cathy was playful and irritated Heathcliff so much that he became violent to her, particularly when Joseph drew his attention to the new relationship between Cathy and Hareton. However, gazing at Cathy's face seemed to prevent him from striking her. Hareton would not allow Cathy to complain of Heathcliff to him; she stopped when she realised his affection for Heathcliff and went on teaching him to read. Heathcliff found them at it, sent them away, and confided to Ellen that he no longer had the energy to destroy the two houses, of the Lintons and the Earnshaws, though it was in his power. All he could think of was Catherine, even breathing was an effort to him; he yearned towards being reunited with her in death.

NOTES AND GLOSSARY:

on the head of it:	on that count
yah . . . yoak:	you may put up with what she does
shoo . . . nob'dy:	she cannot steal anyone's soul away
quean:	girl
een:	eyes
brusts:	bursts
E:	I
set:	plant
mattock:	tool for loosening hard ground

Volume II Chapter 20

For several days after that Heathcliff avoided meals and ate very little; once he was out all night and when he returned he looked excited and glad, though haggard. Every time he began to eat he stopped before he had put food into his mouth. That evening Ellen took him supper and was frightened by his sinister appearance, and again he refused to eat. It made her wonder whether he was supernatural, and where he had come from. The following day when he was alone with Ellen she realised that he was gazing at something he could see but she could not; the implication of what he said later was that he could see Catherine. He was up all night talking to her; the following day he gave instructions about his funeral to Ellen. Two mornings later she was out in the garden early and saw the window of Heathcliff's room (the one where Lockwood had slept and where Heathcliff and Catherine slept as children) swinging open though it was raining hard. She went in and found him dead in the panel bed he had shared with Catherine. He seemed to smile and his wrist was grazed by the window. Only Hareton was deeply moved by his death, and the doctor could not give a cause for Heathcliff's death. Joseph and other villagers claimed to have seen the ghosts of Heathcliff and Catherine.

Just as Ellen reaches this point in her story Hareton and Cathy, who are to be married on New Year's Day and live in the Grange, return from their walk and Lockwood slips away. He walks past the decaying church and the three graves, and wonders that anyone could imagine the dead not sleeping peacefully there.

NOTES AND GLOSSARY:

ghoul:	an evil spirit that robs graves and preys on corpses
vampire:	an evil preternatural being that sucks the blood of sleeping people
they refused . . . Kirk:	a suicide could not be buried on holy ground
the lattice, flapping to and fro:	there was a folk-belief that the window of a dead person's room must be open to release the soul
rare and pleased:	very pleased
Titan:	a giant
chuck:	a term of endearment
harried:	carried
girning:	grinning
remembrance:	souvenir (in this case money)

Part 3

Commentary

Melodrama and sentimentality in romantic novels

As some of the anecdotes in the Introduction indicate, Emily Brontë was self-disciplined and even harsh. She was once bitten by a rabid dog and seared the wound herself with red-hot irons, telling no one about it until she was out of danger. Yet one of the pitfalls for a romantic imagination like hers was the danger of self-indulgence. Many of the situations in the Gondal saga are absurdly melodramatic, giving way to uncontrolled fantasy; it resembles in parts the excesses of the Gothic novel. The Gothic novelists wrote tales of horror, superstition and mystery, often involving monks, nuns and aristocrats, set in the past and taking place in ruined castles among wild mountains and ravines; one of the earliest and most influential was Mrs Radcliffe's *The Mysteries of Udolpho* published in 1794. Jane Austen, writing fifty years before Emily Brontë, had been amused by the excessive sentimentality of Gothic novelists and had satirised it in *Northanger Abbey*. In that novel the heroine is addicted to such Gothic novels as *The Mysteries of Udolpho* and imagines her host at Northanger Abbey to be guilty of unspeakable crimes, whereas he is in fact an ordinary family man. Jane Austen poked fun at the vulnerable heroines of Gothic novels in an early work, *Love and Friendship*, a novel written in letters:

> Never did I see such an affecting Scene as was the meeting of Edward and Augustus.
> 'My Life! my Soul!' (exclaimed the former) 'My Adorable Angel!' (replied the latter) as they flew into each other's arms. It was too pathetic for the feelings of Sophia and myself – We fainted Alternately on a Sofa. (Letter the 8th).

There is an echo in *Wuthering Heights* of a melodramatic story that was published in *Blackwood's Magazine* in 1840, which Emily Brontë might well have read:

> By the side of Ellen Nugent's new-made grave sat the murderer Lawlor, enclosing in his arms the form that had once comprised all earth's love and beauty for him, and which, like a miser, with wild and

maniac affection, he had unburied once more to clasp and contemplate. The shroud had fallen from the upper part of the body, upon which decay had as yet made slight impression. The delicate head lay reclined upon that . . . shoulder which had been its home so often, and over which now streamed the long bright hair like a flood of loosened gold . . . The strangers who dug his grave did not venture to separate in death the hapless pair who in life could never be united.*

This resembles Heathcliff's account of how he opened Catherine's coffin, but this story is too crude to make a lasting impact on the reader; it is a potentially horrifying scene weakened by the stereotyped long golden hair of the heroine and the sentimental language in such phrases as 'the hapless pair', which enables us to dismiss it as a fairy story. And yet it does embody a part of human nature that exists and merits serious expression; there is considerable difficulty in creating in fiction a character so dominated by one consuming passion that he does not feel the normal human aversion to physical decay, as it can easily slip into seeming melodramatic or sentimental.

These critical terms 'melodramatic' and 'sentimental' have to be used carefully of the Victorian novel. The many lingering deaths, particularly of children, in Victorian fiction are sometimes described as examples of melodramatic sentimentality but this shows the critic's failure to grasp that the Victorian world was not the same as ours. Sudden death from typhoid fever or cholera and lingering fatal diseases such as tuberculosis were part of the texture of life for the Victorians; their invalids were nursed at home and the pain of watching them suffer was intensified by their inability to alleviate the suffering with pain-killing drugs. A Victorian reader might legitimately complain that a novel was incredible if there were not a few sudden or infant deaths in it. Victorian domestic life abounded in drama and pathos; whether these qualities are rendered melodramatic and sentimental in novels depends on the treatment of the events recorded rather than on the nature of the events themselves; that is to say that the lingering death of a child, like Linton Heathcliff, in a Victorian novel is not intrinsically sentimental since it was a common part of Victorian experience but the rendering of it by the novelist, the excessive indulgence in emotion, can make it sentimental rather than pathetic. In *Wuthering Heights* Emily Brontë has two difficulties to overcome: she has the problem common to most Victorian novelists of dealing with domestic life, subject matter that is potentially melodramatic and sentimental, and the peculiar problem of treating Heathcliff's extraordinary but not incredible passion for Catherine.

*Quoted in the Clarendon Press edition of *Wuthering Heights* p. 431

Structure of the novel

Narrative method

If we consider the treatment of a consumptive character in *Wuthering Heights* the distinction between potentially sentimental material and the actual effect on the reader of a passage becomes clear.

> I did remark, to be sure, that mounting the stairs made her breathe very quick, that the least sudden noise set her all in a quiver, and that she coughed troublesomely sometimes: but I knew nothing of what these symptoms portended, and had no impulse to sympathise with her. We don't in general take to foreigners here, Mr Lockwood, unless they take to us first. (Chapter 6)*

As readers we cannot wallow in tears for Frances because her illness is not described emotively by the author, but dismissively by Ellen. Ellen and Lockwood as narrators are crucial to the success of *Wuthering Heights*.

There is a detailed study in Part 4 of the role of Lockwood in the novel; Emily Brontë knew how strange Yorkshire would seem to most of her contemporaries and used Lockwood who was also a stranger to it to record his impressions of it. At the same time she manipulates our sympathies through Lockwood; he is such an affected prig that we are drawn to Catherine by being moved from Lockwood's sneering pedantic language to a vigorous past relived in Catherine's diary.

> I began, forthwith, to decypher her faded hieroglyphics.
> 'An awful Sunday!' commenced the paragraph beneath. 'I wish my father were back again. Hindley is a detestable substitute – his conduct to Heathcliff is atrocious – H. and I are going to rebel.' (Chapter 3)

This contrasts sharply with Lockwood's own diary in which it is enclosed.

The key question about the narrative method of *Wuthering Heights* is why Emily Brontë uses Ellen Dean as the main narrator of the novel, and the answer lies in her awareness of the possible hazards suggested at the beginning of this section. The story she wants to tell might seem incredible if an omniscient narrator told it directly but Emily Brontë weaves into the story with unprecedented complexity, protecting the reader from the full impact of the violent passions in the novel. We come to everything through Ellen Dean, and the most important aspect of her character is her ordinariness. Catherine is undoubtedly an irritating

*As most modern editions of *Wuthering Heights* disregard the division into two volumes and number the chapters from 1–34, this is also done in Parts 3 and 4

character but Ellen is so resolutely unsympathetic with her in the most intense moments of her suffering that our irritation with her is deflected and we feel what Ellen does not.

> 'No!' she shrieked. 'Oh, don't, don't go. It is the last time! Edgar will not hurt us. Heathcliff, I shall die! I shall die!'
> 'Damn the fool. There he is,' cried Heathcliff, sinking back into his seat. 'Hush, my darling!' ... In the midst of my agitation, I was sincerely glad to observe that Catherine's arms had fallen relaxed, and her head hung down.
> 'She's fainted or dead,' I thought, 'so much the better. Far better that she should be dead, than lingering a burden and a misery-maker to all about her.' (Chapter 15)

Another aspect of this scene is the way in which Ellen is unperturbed by the violence of the emotions expressed; she mutters about it but she rarely seems really shocked, and this has a cushioning effect for the reader.

Through her, wild passions become rooted in the normality of domestic life; as a servant she notices domestic details and can comment on them in a way that would seem trivial in another narrator, as for example in the scene when Heathcliff entices Cathy and Ellen to the Heights and locks them in.

> Cathy ran to me instead of Linton, and knelt down, and put her burning cheek on my lap, weeping aloud ... Mr Heathcliff, perceiving us all confounded, rose, and expeditiously made the tea himself. The cups and saucers were laid ready. He poured it out, and handed me a cup. (Chapter 27)

We do not expect Ghouls to make tea; Heathcliff is made part of recognisable reality through the servant's memory of being waited on, and her observation that he had probably prepared the tea himself.

Above all, she comments on the action but is unreliable as a commentator; she says of Edgar and Catherine:

> I believe I may assert that they were really in possession of deep and growing happiness.
> It ended. Well, we *must* be for ourselves in the long run; the mild and generous are only more justly selfish than the domineering – and it ended when circumstances caused each to feel that the one's interest was not the chief consideration in the other's thoughts. (Chapter 10)

We assume she has never been in love; through this kind of comment she reveals her inability to understand what Heathcliff is capable of giving up for Catherine. The reader cannot trust her interpretation of events although she has so much common sense. She says of herself:

> I seated myself in a chair, and rocked, to and fro, passing harsh judgment on my many derelictions of duty; from which, it struck me then, all the misfortunes of all my employers sprang. It was not the case, in reality, I am aware; but it was, in my imagination, that dismal night, and I thought Heathcliff himself less guilty than I. (Chapter 27)

In one sense this could be said to be true; she is so unsympathetic with Catherine, confessing that she does not like her, that she could have precipitated Heathcliff's disappearance and Catherine's fatal illness.

Her superstition is another aspect of her character of which the reader has to be wary; she wonders gloomily whether Heathcliff is a ghoul or a vampire, and where he came from, '"the little dark thing, harboured by a good man to his bane."' (Chapter 34) We cannot trust Ellen's memory here; Heathcliff gave Mr Earnshaw pleasure and though he assisted Hindley's loss of dignity and property he was not responsible for it; Hindley's grief over Frances's death was what made him degenerate, so Heathcliff was not responsible for the destruction of the Earnshaw fortunes.

Ellen serves a double purpose: to give a credible realistic framework to the extraordinary story but also to force the reader to evaluate every event for himself because he cannot trust her judgement.

Setting

A crucial part of the realistic framework Ellen provides for the reader is observation of domestic and seasonal detail. She is a countrywoman who is attuned to the significance of changes in the weather, whose senses are alert, and whose life is governed by the routine of domestic and farm life:

> We were busy with the hay in a far-away field, when the girl that usually brought our breakfasts came running, an hour too soon, across the meadow and up the lane. (Chapter 8)

Her comments on her surroundings inform us about them on a literal level and at the same time often contribute to the development of themes in the novel. Just before Catherine's last fatal encounter with Heathcliff she sits listening to the stream:

> Gimmerton chapel bells were still ringing; and the full, mellow flow of the beck in the valley came soothingly on the ear. It was a sweet substitute for the yet absent murmur of the summer foliage, which drowned that music about the Grange when the trees were in leaf. At Wuthering Heights it always sounded on quiet days, following a great thaw, or a season of steady rain – and of Wuthering Heights Catherine was thinking as she listened. (Chapter 15)

When Ellen comments on this sound again, Heathcliff is close to his death, and the sound of the beck hints at the mysterious bond there is between him and Catherine:

> The room was filled with the damp, mild air of the cloudy evening, and so still, that not only the murmur of the beck down Gimmerton was distinguishable, but its ripples and its gurglings over the pebbles, or through the large stones which it could not cover. (Chapter 34)

Ellen's intimate knowledge of the Heights and the Grange is used to give us a vivid sense of the life in each place. There is a symbolic suggestion about the two places: the Heights is exposed to the elements and the home of wild passions while the more civilised Grange is in a sheltered valley and appropriate for the gentle affection Edgar feels for his wife and daughter. But Ellen's pride in her work gives us a fuller picture of the Heights; it acquires the texture of reality for the reader.

Because Ellen shifts to and from the Grange and the Heights with her two mistresses we get to know the internal workings of each place and the relative merits of each. We cannot easily dismiss one place in favour of the other; we see, with Ellen, the Heights from the Grange and know why Catherine longs to be in the Heights during her last illness, but we understand equally well why Isabella cannot bear the Heights and longs for the Grange. Their difference is the important factor, but in its own way the Heights is as attractive as the Grange; indeed in the second chapter Lockwood leaves his dusty hearth at the Grange for the 'large, warm, cheerful apartment' with 'the radiance of an immense fire' at the Heights. He immediately encounters the converse situation in Catherine's diary; she and Heathcliff escape from the cold and damp of the Heights and, we discover later, are drawn to the Grange, '"a splendid place carpeted with crimson, and crimson-covered chairs and tables, and a pure white ceiling bordered by gold."' (Chapter 6)

Time-scheme and plot

Whatever element of the structure of *Wuthering Heights* is discussed, the function of the narrator in it has always to be considered. If we were to isolate Catherine Earnshaw from the novel and analyse her character we might find her unappealing, but as we read we are manipulated by the form of the book into sympathising with her. Our first impression of her is not in chronological order: we meet her first when Lockwood reads her diary. She is twelve and she and Heathcliff are victims of her brother's cruelty. When Ellen starts her story she describes Catherine as a wilful smaller child but we retain a sense of her vulnerability, and of the mutual dependence between her and Heathcliff.

The relationship that dominates the book is clearly that between

Heathcliff and Catherine, and yet, if the story were told in strict chronological order, it would end with the love between Hareton and Cathy. By making use of Lockwood and Ellen, Emily Brontë disrupts the chronological sequence of events to give prominence to the thematically crucial moments in the novel: the evening when Heathcliff and Catherine first see the Grange, their separation, the death of Catherine and the death of Heathcliff.

When Lockwood reads about the scàmper on the moors in Catherine's diary we do not know the full significance of it, but when Ellen reaches the part of her narrative describing Heathcliff's and Catherine's Sunday evening exploit in the sixth chapter, we make the connection and so pay particular attention to Heathcliff's account of how they looked through the windows of the Grange. The immediacy of the scene is highlighted by the fact that it is told in Heathcliff's own words, reported to Lockwood by Ellen; Cathy, Isabella and Zillah tell their parts of the story with similar directness later. The next milestone in the story is the separation of Catherine and Heathcliff, and Emily Brontë encourages the reader to pause and dwell on its implications by making Ellen break off her story immediately after it so that Lockwood can go to bed. Catherine's death comes after another such moment, in the first chapter of the second volume, halfway through the novel.

Emily Brontë makes use of both narrators to ensure that Heathcliff's death and the suggestion of his reunion with Catherine come at the end of the book. Lockwood returns to Yorkshire after an absence of several months, and the first thing that he sees when he reaches the Heights is the loving intimacy between Hareton and Cathy. This disposes of the reader's curiosity about them and allows him to focus on the central issue: what has happened to Heathcliff? Lockwood then finds Ellen and tells of Heathcliff's strange death in her usual prosaic way, and the book ends with the three graves, not with the young lovers.

There is an unusual symmetry about the plot, which is best shown by a genealogical table.

Mr Earnshaw	m.	Mrs Earnshaw				Mr Linton	m.	Mrs Linton	
d. October 1777		d. spring 1773				d. autumn 1780			

Hindley	m.	Frances	Catherine	m.	Edgar	Isabella	m.	Heathcliff
b. summer 1757	(1777)	d. late 1778	b. summer 1765	(spring	b. 1762	b. late 1765	(Jan. 1784)	b. 1764
d. September 1784			d. 20 March 1784	1783)	d. September 1801	d. summer 1797		d. May 1802

Hareton	m.	Catherine	m.	Linton
b. June 1778	(1 January 1803)	b. 20 March 1784	(September 1801)	b. September 1784
				d. September 1801

There are two sets of brothers and sisters, Hindley and Catherine Earnshaw and Edgar and Isabella Linton, one belonging to the Heights and the other to the Grange. The two houses come together in the marriage of Catherine and Edgar, and of Isabella and Heathcliff; Hindley's son, Hareton, is also the product of a union between the wildness of the Heights (Hindley) and the civilised world to which the Lintons belong (Frances). Cathy marries first Linton Heathcliff, then Hareton, resolving the family connections into one single marriage.

This pattern is heightened by the repetition of names; there seems a wilful confusion about the repetition of the name Catherine in the second generation and in calling Isabella's son Linton Heathcliff. Why does the author do it, and why does she draw our attention to the names?

> This writing, however, was nothing but a name repeated in all kinds of characters, large and small – *Catherine Earnshaw*, here and there varied to *Catherine Heathcliff*, and then again to *Catherine Linton*.
>
> In vapid listlessness I leant my head against the window, and continued spelling over Catherine Earnshaw-Heathcliff-Linton, till my eyes closed; but they had not rested five minutes when a glare of white letters started from the dark, as vivid as spectres – the air swarmed with Catherines. (Chapter 3)

We may be inclined to feel that the air swarms with Catherines by the time we finish reading the novel for the first time, but in fact the plot itself helps us to understand the meaning of the book.

Stated baldly, it is Catherine Earnshaw who causes all the trouble. She marries Edgar Linton for the wrong reasons, knowing that she should have married Heathcliff. Emily Brontë's purpose in using the name Cathy for the first Catherine's daughter is to show the damage one generation does to the subsequent one. Catherine's marriage causes the unnatural union of Heathcliff and Isabella; Heathcliff hates Isabella and marries her only to have his revenge on Edgar. Their child is called Linton Heathcliff to symbolise the impossibility of the marriage. Within the terms of the book Linton and Heathcliff are incompatible, and Linton Heathcliff's frailty shows that they cannot co-exist. Cathy marries her cousin and becomes Catherine Heathcliff, the name her mother might have had. The first Catherine's sin is still not expiated, however, and harmony is only restored when she and Hareton are to be married. When they fall in love Heathcliff recognises himself and Catherine in them; both pairs of names begin with H and C. He begins to be haunted by the image of the first Catherine, and through the marriage of Cathy and Hareton he is free to be reunited, at least physically and possibly spiritually, with Catherine. With Cathy's marriage there will be a Catherine Earnshaw again and the wheel will have come full circle.

The appearance of the ghost to Lockwood at the beginning sets us a puzzle that we cannot solve until the end of the novel: a puzzle to which Lockwood himself draws our attention:

> My fingers closed on the fingers of a little, ice-cold hand!
> The intense horror of nightmare came over me; I tried to draw back my arm, but the hand clung to it, and a most melancholy voice sobbed,
> 'Let me in – let me in!'
> 'Who are you?' I asked, struggling, meanwhile, to disengage myself.
> 'Catherine Linton,' it replied, shiveringly (why did I think of *Linton*? I had read *Earnshaw* twenty times for Linton). 'I'm come home, I'd lost my way on the moor! . . . I've been a waif for twenty years!' (Chapter 3)

The scene is a chilling one partly because Lockwood is such an unimaginative, urbane man; the ghost has a vividness for the reader that it would not have if it had appeared to a superstitious woman like Ellen. The puzzle, which becomes more of a puzzle as the novel progresses, is why the child calls herself Catherine Linton; when she was a child she was called Catherine Earnshaw. Another difficulty is why she says she has been a waif for twenty years when she has only been dead for seventeen years, and the chronology of the book is faultlessly accurate throughout.

We might wonder if it was her marriage that made her a waif, yet this had taken place eighteen, not twenty, years before. The explanation lies in the scene when Catherine is delirious in the Grange; Ellen says of her that 'our fiery Catherine was no better than a wailing child' and this reminds the reader of Lockwood's ghost which 'wailed'. Catherine in her frenzy goes on:

> 'But supposing at twelve years old I had been wrenched from the Heights, and every early association, and my all in all, as Heathcliff was at that time, and been converted at a stroke into Mrs Linton, the lady of Thrushcross Grange, and the wife of a stranger; an exile, and outcast, thenceforth, from what had been my world – You may fancy a glimpse of the abyss where I grovelled!' (Chapter 12)

Just over twenty years elapsed between the time that Catherine tells Ellen, in the kitchen at the Heights, that she has decided to marry Edgar and the time that Lockwood sees the ghost in his dream. In accepting Edgar she accepts social advancement and rejects the love she feels for Heathcliff: she accepts the world of the Grange and cuts herself off from the Heights, and Heathcliff runs away. This precipitates all the subsequent disasters. She should not be a Linton and while the effects of what she has done are still goading Heathcliff on to revenge, she is shut out of the Heights: Heathcliff begs her to come in but she cannot. Only when her daughter is about to become Catherine Earnshaw can the ghostly waif get in. Heathcliff dies in the room where he used to sleep with Catherine as a child, and where Lockwood saw the ghost, and the suggestion is that the ghost comes for Heathcliff, as the detail of the grazed hand echoes the earlier scene and his look of exultation implies that he must have achieved what he had desired.

> I could not think him dead – but his face and throat were washed with rain; the bed-clothes dripped, and he was perfectly still. The lattice, flapping to and fro, had grazed one hand that rested on the sill – no blood trickled from the broken skin, and when I put my fingers to it, I could doubt no more – he was dead and stark!
> I hasped the window; I combed his black long hair from his forehead; I tried to close his eyes – to extinguish, if possible, that frightful, life-like gaze of exultation, before anyone else beheld it. (Chapter 34)

Joseph and the local people claim to have seen the dead Catherine and Heathcliff inside the house.

> There are those who speak to having met him near the church, and on the moor, and even within this house – Idle tales, you'll say, and so say I. Yet that old man by the kitchen fire affirms he has seen the two on 'em, looking out of his chamber window, on every rainy night since his death. (Chapter 34)

Characters

Catherine

Catherine is clearly wayward from girlhood; Ellen describes her before her father's death as 'a wild wick slip'. (Chapter 5)

Emily Brontë sustains the sense that we have of Catherine's high spirits throughout the novel: when Heathcliff returns after his long absence she is too excited to sleep and is annoyed by Edgar's sullenness. She is also feminine in her pleasure in her new clothes when she returns from her first visit to the Lintons, and she does not want Heathcliff to soil them. Ellen thinks she has changed towards Heathcliff and that she does not care that he is locked up on Christmas Day, but soon finds she is wrong.

Catherine remains faithful to all her early affections; Ellen says that she did not like Catherine but that Catherine never turned against her. Catherine develops a double standard to accommodate her feelings for both Edgar and Heathcliff as Hindley degrades Heathcliff more and more; Ellen says 'she was full of ambition' and was anxious to ingratiate herself with the Lintons.

The scene in which this duality reaches its climax is her confession to Ellen that she has accepted Edgar. Dreams are used to convey meaning to the reader in *Wuthering Heights*, as has been suggested about Lockwood's dream; here Catherine describes her dream of being in heaven:

> 'I was only going to say that heaven did not seem to be my home; and I broke my heart with weeping to come back to earth; and the angels were so angry that they flung me out, into the middle of the heath on the top of Wuthering Heights; where I woke sobbing for joy. That will do to explain my secret, as well as the other. I've no more business to marry Edgar Linton than I have to be in heaven.' (Chapter 9)

She knows that she loves Edgar with a superficial affection, for his looks, and because 'he will be rich, and I shall like to be the greatest woman of the neighbourhood'. She emphasises her love for Heathcliff in almost religious terms:

> 'But surely you and everybody have a notion that there is, or should be, an existence of yours beyond you. What were the use of my creation if I were entirely contained here? My great miseries in this world have been Heathcliff's miseries, and I watched and felt each from the beginning; my great thought in living is himself. If all else perished, and *he* remained, I should still continue to be; and, if all else remained, and he were annihilated, the Universe would turn to a mighty stranger.' (Chapter 9)

Her attitude to the Heights and the moors suggest that she should never have become part of the civilised world, and knows that she should not; her heaven is at the Heights and her spiritual experience inextricable from Heathcliff. Ellen says to her that she was responsible for Heathcliff's disappearance but because of her illness she has to be humoured more than ever. The other direct result of what we have to see within the framework of the novel as her sin is the death of Edgar's parents, who catch the fever from Catherine and die of it.

When Heathcliff returns after her marriage Catherine shows that she will not accept the blame for their situations; she is petulant with Edgar because he does not welcome Heathcliff and pretends that she has not ill-treated Heathcliff, though he describes her accurately as a tyrant:

> 'How have I treated you infernally?'
> 'I seek no revenge on you,' replied Heathcliff less vehemently. 'That's not the plan – The tyrant grinds down his slaves – and they don't turn against him, they crush those beneath them. You are

welcome to torture me to death for your amusement, only, allow me to amuse myself a little in the same style.' (Chapter 11)

After an angry scene between Edgar and Heathcliff, Catherine can still say, 'I am in no way blameable in this matter' but she also says something more ominous. She is so determined to have her own way that she is ready to die to get it:

> 'Well, if I cannot keep Heathcliff for my friend – if Edgar will be mean and jealous – I'll try to break their hearts by breaking my own. That will be a prompt way of finishing all, when I am pushed to extremity!'

This is precisely what she does, driven on by Ellen who totally misunderstands how ill she is. After locking herself in her room for three days she becomes delirious, but reaches new understanding:

> 'But I begin to fancy you don't like me. How strange! I thought, though everybody hated and despised each other, they could not avoid loving me – and they have all turned to enemies in a few hours.' (Chapter 12)

She decides that the only way back to the Heights is through breaking her own heart, through suicide:

> 'It's a rough journey, and a sad heart to travel it; and we must pass by Gimmerton Kirk, to go that journey! We've braved its ghosts often together, and dared each other to stand among the graves and ask them to come . . . But Heathcliff, if I dare you now, will you venture? If you do, I'll keep you . . . I won't rest till you are with me . . . He's considering . . . he'd rather I'd come to him! Find a way, then! not through that Kirkyard . . . You are slow! Be content, you always followed me!'

She leans out of the window, deliberately chilling herself while she is feverish, and when Edgar appears she tells him that she no longer needs him as she will soon be dead. Heathcliff understands exactly what she has done and forces her to be truthful; at first she says, during the last afternoon of her life, that he has killed her but eventually she acknowledges, 'You never harmed me in your life.' He sums up:

> '*Why* did you betray your own heart, Cathy? I have not one word of comfort – you deserve this. You have killed yourself. Yes, you may kiss me, and cry; and wring out my kisses and tears. They'll blight you – they'll damn you. You loved me – what *right* had you to leave me? What right – answer me – for the poor fancy you felt for Linton? Because misery, and degradation, and death, and nothing that God or Satan could inflict would have parted us, *you*, of your own will, did it. I have not broken your heart – *you* have broken it – and in breaking it, you have broken mine.' (Chapter 15)

She has killed herself to escape from the intolerable situation that she herself created, and the reader is asked to consider what she does in spiritual terms, for the language Heathcliff uses is religious: he employs such words as 'damn', 'God', 'Satan', 'soul'.

Heathcliff

Catherine is morally responsible for all the evil in the novel except Hindley's ill-treatment of Hareton. This is particularly important as no one in the novel fully understands it, and Charlotte Brontë obviously did not either. She, like Ellen, seems to have been deceived by the language that is constantly used of him. When Mr Earnshaw brings him home at first he says he is 'as dark almost as if it came from the devil.' This is a superstitious idea which remains with Ellen, so that she wonders at the end, 'Where did he come from, the little dark thing, harboured by a good man to his bane?' When Isabella writes to Ellen she asks 'Is he a devil?', Hindley calls him a 'fiend' and a 'hellish villain' and Catherine compares him to Satan. Yet only Catherine really understands his character; she interprets it for Isabella:

'Tell her what Heathcliff is – an unreclaimed creature, without refinement – without cultivation; an arid wilderness of furze and whinstone. I'd as soon put that little canary into the park on a winter's day as recommend you to bestow your heart on him! . . . Pray don't imagine that he conceals depths of benevolence and affection beneath a stern exterior! He's not a rough diamond – a pearl-containing oyster of a rustic; he's a fierce, pitiless, wolfish man.' (Chapter 10)

What Catherine is describing is the reality behind the Byronic hero. Heathcliff has all the attributes of such a hero; the first impression he gives Lockwood (and thus ourselves as readers) is that he is magnetic, powerful, handsome and melancholy. The other, unpalatable side of his character, his savagery, brutality and dishonesty, is also made clear and the two combine to create his mysterious fascination.

Emily Brontë's hero is fully Romantic, for she makes it clear that Heathcliff's unorthodox devotion of the self to one consuming passion can have ugly and frightening results. From his childhood he never forgot an injury, and the systematic and materialistic way in which he goes about contriving his revenge on Hindley is chilling. His courtship of Isabella is peculiarly repellent, as is the way in which he experiments on her feelings after their marriage:

'Now, was it not the depth of absurdity – of genuine idiocy, for that pitiful, slavish, mean-minded brach to dream that I could love her? Tell your master, Nelly, that I never, in all my life, met with such an abject thing as she is – She even disgraces the name of Linton; and I've

sometimes relented, from pure lack of invention, in my experiments
on what she could endure, and still creep shamefully cringing back!'
(Chapter 14)

He is intelligent and understands what has caused Isabella's infatuation:

'She abandoned them under a delusion . . . picturing in me a hero of
romance, and expecting unlimited indulgences from my chivalrous
devotion. I can hardly regard her in the light of a rational creature, so
obstinately has she persisted in forming a fabulous notion of my
character, and acting on the false impressions she cherished.'
(Chapter 14)

Heathcliff is a Romantic hero realistically presented; there is no glamour
about his account of how he dug up Catherine's coffin and certainly
none about his treatment of Hindley and Linton Heathcliff which is
squalid and disgusting. He speaks the truth when he says he has no pity,
but the superhuman aspect of him is his love for Catherine which is total
and unselfish even when he is a child, and is maintained into adulthood:

'Had he been in my place, and I in his, though I hated him with a
hatred that turned my life to gall, I never would have raised a hand
against him. You may look incredulous, if you please! I never would
have banished him from her society, as long as she desired his. The
moment her regard ceased, I would have torn his heart out, and drunk
his blood! But, till then – if you don't believe me, you don't know
me – till then, I would have died by inches before I touched a single
hair of his head!' (Chapter 14)

In spite of his physical strength, she dominates him throughout the
novel. In her delirium, she dares him to follow her through death to
reunion, and he tells Ellen how his life is as much dominated by her after
her death as it was before:

'What does not recall her? I cannot look down to this floor, but her
features are shaped on the flags! In every cloud, in every tree – filling
the air at night, and caught by glimpses in every object by day, I am
surrounded with her image! The most ordinary faces of men and
women – my own features – mock me with a resemblance. The entire
world is a dreadful collection of memoranda that she did exist, and
that I have lost her . . . I have a single wish, and my whole being and
faculties are yearning to attain it. They have yearned towards it so
long, and so unwaveringly, that I'm convinced it *will* be reached – and
soon – because it has devoured my existence – I am swallowed in the
anticipation of its fulfilment.' (Chapter 33)

There is nothing sentimental about his wish to mingle his dust with
Catherine's because it is not an idle fantasy; he has opened her coffin

after eighteen years and looked at her decaying corpse, and knows what
he is saying:

> 'I dreamt I was sleeping the last sleep, by that sleeper, with my heart
> stopped, and my cheek frozen against hers.'
> 'And if she had been dissolved into earth, or worse, what would you
> have dreamt of then?' I said.
> 'Of dissolving with her, and being more happy still! . . . Do you
> suppose I dread any change of that sòrt? I expected such a
> transformation on raising the lid, but I'm better pleased that it should
> not commence till I share it.' (Chapter 29)

There is something elemental about him and Catherine; he is first
associated with the elements through the description of his house:

> 'Wuthering Heights is the name of Mr Heathcliff's dwelling,
> 'Wuthering' being a significant provincial adjective, descriptive of the
> atmospheric tumult to which its station is exposed in stormy weather.
> Pure, bracing ventilation they must have up there, at all times, indeed:
> one may guess the power of the north wind, blowing over the edge, by
> the excessive slant of a few, stunted firs at the end of the house; and by
> a range of gaunt thorns all stretching their limbs one way, as if craving
> alms of the sun. (Chapter 1)

He is connected here, as in the passage when Catherine describes his
character to Isabella and in his name itself, with the harsh aspects of
nature, with thorns, the north wind, cliffs, a wilderness of furze and
whinstone, winter and wolves. After Catherine's death Ellen finds him
and says that he seems part of the natural not of the civilised world:

> 'He was there – at least a few yards further in the park; leant against
> an old ash tree, his hat off, and his hair soaked with the dew that had
> gathered on the budded branches, and fell pattering round him. He
> had been standing a long time in that position, for I saw a pair of
> ousels passing and repassing scarcely three feet from him, busy in
> building their nest, and regarding his proximity no more than that of a
> piece of timber. (Chapter 16)

His funeral is in keeping with this:

> 'You remind me of the manner that I desire to be buried in – It is to be
> carried to the churchyard, in the evening. You and Hareton may, if
> you please, accompany me – and mind, particularly, to notice that the
> sexton obeys my directions concerning the two coffins! No minister
> need come; nor need anything be said over me – I tell you, I have
> nearly attained *my* heaven; and that of others is altogether unvalued
> and uncoveted by me!' (Chapter 34)

Ellen says that they knew none of the normal details that are written on
headstones in a graveyard and could only inscribe on it 'Heathcliff'.

Edgar

Edgar represents the world of conventional morality which Heathcliff rejects:

> 'And that insipid, paltry creature attending her from *duty* and *humanity*! From *pity and charity*! He might as well plant an oak in a flower-pot, and expect it to thrive, as imagine he can restore her to vigour in the soil of his shallow cares!' (Chapter 14)

What Heathcliff says about Edgar is right up to a point; certainly, in the first part of the novel, when the reader is in the world of the Heights, Edgar seems a feeble character. Lockwood's admiration of Edgar's portrait confirms the reader's suspicion of Edgar's weakness as Lockwood is so unerringly mistaken in every judgement he attempts. The image Ellen uses to describe him in the following passage even implies that there is something sick in Edgar's attraction to Catherine:

> The soft thing looked askance through the window – he possessed the power to depart, as much as a cat possesses the power to leave a mouse half killed, or a bird half eaten. (Chapter 8)

However, when the action transfers to the Grange the reader sees the refinement of the Grange in a different light. Edgar has a moral strength which grows as Heathcliff torments him. He too yearns for death and reunion with Catherine. His lack of vindictiveness is not frailty but humane unselfishness. His death is as dignified and moving as his life has become; like Heathcliff he dies thinking of Catherine:

> 'I am going to her, and you, darling child, shall come to us,' and never stirred or spoke again, but continued that rapt, radiant gaze, till his pulse imperceptibly stopped, and his soul departed. (Chapter 28)

Isabella

Isabella does not attain to Edgar's moral stature in the novel though she shares his less attractive qualities. They are compared unfavourably with Heathcliff and Catherine by Heathcliff himself:

> 'Isabella – I believe she is eleven, a year younger than Cathy – lay screaming at the farther end of the room, shrieking as if witches were running red hot needles into her. Edgar stood on the hearth weeping silently, and in the middle of the table sat a little dog, shaking its paw and yelping, which, from their mutual accusations, we understood they had nearly pulled in two between them. The idiots! That was their pleasure!' (Chapter 6)

Isabella's infatuation with Heathcliff does not grow into unselfish devotion as Edgar's for Catherine does, and its roots are distasteful, as Heathcliff points out:

'She cannot accuse me of showing a bit of deceitful softness. The first thing she saw me do, on coming out of the Grange, was to hang up her little dog, and when she pleaded for it the first words I uttered were the wish that I had the hanging of every being belonging to her, except one: possibly she took that exception for herself – But no brutality disgusted her – I suppose she has an innate admiration of it, if only her precious person were secure from injury!' (Chapter 14)

She is fascinated by brutality and is stupid. She never understands the relationship between Heathcliff and Catherine and never quite recognises her fantasy about him for what it is:

'I've recovered from my first desire to be killed by him. I'd rather he'd kill himself! He has extinguished my love effectually, and so I'm at my ease. I can recollect yet how I loved him; and can dimly imagine that I could still be loving him, if – No, no! (Chapter 17)

Linton Heathcliff

Isabella's son seems the fitting product of an unnatural union; he combines Isabella's slavishness with Heathcliff's cruelty:

'Linton was white and trembling. He was not pretty then, Ellen – Oh, no! he looked frightful! for his thin face and large eyes were wrought into an expression of frantic, powerless fury. He grasped the handle of the door, and shook it – it was fastened inside.

    'If you don't let me in I'll kill you! If you don't let me in I'll kill you! . . . Devil! devil!' (Chapter 24)

This passage might suggest that he is insufficiently credible as a character, that he is only a walking symbol, but this suggestion is not borne out by the reader's experience, partly because Linton's vicious powerlessness is brought so vividly alive but also because in his better moments he recognises his own character.

'I *am* worthless, and bad in temper, and bad in spirit, almost always . . . Believe that if I might be as sweet, and as kind, and as good as you are, I would be, as willingly, and more so, than as happy and as healthy. And believe that your kindness has made me love you deeper than if I deserved your love, and though I couldn't, and cannot help showing my nature to you, I regret and repent it, and shall regret and repent it, till I die!' (Chapter 24)

Cathy

There is a strong sense of heredity in *Wuthering Heights*; Ellen sees both her parents in Cathy. In her combination of qualities she is much more ordinary than her mother; she is brave and high-spirited but not wilful and domineering. She is in every way a normal, rather spoilt girl; when she is pampered she is happy, when she is consistently ill-treated she becomes sullen, and when she is in love she is playful. There is no ardent intensity in the love between Hareton and Cathy as there was between Heathcliff and Catherine:

> Catherine usually sat by me; but today she stole nearer to Hareton . . . The minute after, she had sidled to him, and was sticking primroses in his plate of porridge.
>
> He dared not speak to her, there; he dared hardly look; and yet she went on teasing, till he was twice on the point of being provoked to laugh. (Chapter 33)

She grows with experience; she loses her snobbish contempt for Hareton and respects his love for Heathcliff:

> She showed a good heart, thenceforth, in avoiding both complaints and expressions of antipathy concerning Heathcliff; and confessed to me her sorrow that she had endeavoured to raise a bad spirit between him and Hareton – indeed, I don't believe she has ever breathed a syllable, in the latter's hearing, against her oppressor, since. (Chapter 33)

Hareton

Of the younger generation in the novel Hareton is perhaps the most interesting character, partly because he is in so many ways a mirror image of Heathcliff. To revenge himself on Hindley, even after his death, Heathcliff degrades his son as Hindley had once degraded him:

> 'If he were a born fool I should not enjoy it half so much – But he's no fool; and I can sympathise with all his feelings, having felt them myself – I know what he suffers now, for instance, exactly – it is merely a beginning of what he shall suffer, though. And he'll never be able to emerge from his bathos of coarseness and ignorance. I've got him faster than his scoundrel of a father secured me, and lower; for he takes a pride in his brutishness.' (Chapter 21)

Hareton's attempts to improve himself are as moving as Heathcliff's youthful 'Nelly, make me decent, I'm going to be good.' (Chapter 7) Hareton, too, washes when Cathy comes to visit the Heights, threatens

Linton as Heathcliff once threatended Edgar, and is humiliated by Cathy:

'He looked up to the inscription above, and said, with a stupid mixture of awkwardness and elation:
"Miss Catherine! I can read yon, nah."
"Wonderful!" I exclaimed. "Pray let us hear you – you are grown clever!" . . . The fool stared, with a grin hovering about his lips, and a scowl gathering over his eyes, as if uncertain whether he might not join in my mirth; whether it were not pleasant familiarity, or what it really was, contempt.' (Chapter 24)

He is, however, unlike Heathcliff in his loving generosity:

Poor Hareton, the most wronged, was the only one that really suffered much. He sat by the corpse all night, weeping in bitter earnest. He pressed its hand, and kissed the sarcastic, savage face that everyone else shrank from contemplating; and bemoaned him with that strong grief which springs naturally from a generous heart, though it be tough as tempered steel. (Chapter 34)

He comes to love Cathy, but with a love which resembles Edgar's love for Catherine much more than Heathcliff's; it contains the normal ingredients of physical love which are never mentioned in connection with Heathcliff and Catherine until Catherine is dying:

His handsome features glowed with pleasure, and his eyes kept impatiently wandering from the page to a small white hand over his shoulder . . . The task was done, not free from further blunders, but the pupil claimed a reward, and received at least five kisses, which, however, he generously returned. (Chapter 32)

When they do fall in love they change Heathcliff; Catherine's sin has been exorcised and Heathcliff can see both himself and Catherine in Hareton:

'Hareton's aspect was the ghost of my immortal love, of my wild endeavours to hold my right, my degradation, my pride, my happiness, and my anguish.' (Chapter 33)

Hindley

Hindley belongs at the Heights with Heathcliff and Catherine because he resembles them in many ways. He is spoilt like Catherine, always expecting to get his own way, and grieves for his wife's death with a violence and wholeheartedness that are worthy of Heathcliff:

For himself, he grew desperate; his sorrow was of that kind that will not lament; he neither wept nor prayed – he cursed and defied – execrated God and men, and gave himself up to reckless dissipation. (Chapter 8)

He is as stubborn in his hatred of Heathcliff for usurping his father's affection as Heathcliff is in exacting his revenge for Hindley's degradation of him. There is a strong indication that Heathcliff eventually kills Hindley; Hindley himself is torn between his longing to kill Heathcliff and his wish to win back his money and property from him before he kills him.

Joseph

Joseph also belongs at the Heights in spite of his apparent Christianity; he is uncompromising and cruel. He provides one of the many ideas about life after death that abound in the novel, his being the harsh view that only a few are saved and most perish in hell.

Style

The language of *Wuthering Heights* has a sensuous particularity that conveys a great deal to the reader's imagination; from the first page of the novel clear visual images of how people, houses and landscape look are presented to us. It matters that Heathcliff is tall and swarthy whereas Edgar is fair and slender for this embodies a meaning: they represent two opposed ways of life. Catherine has brown hair and dark eyes like Heathcliff, Isabella is fair and blue-eyed like Edgar, and Cathy, physically as in so many other respects, is a compromise, with fair hair and dark eyes. You may find it useful to compare the first page of *Wuthering Heights* with the first page of a novel by Jane Austen to see how abstract Jane Austen's language is in comparison with Emily Brontë's; we are not given clear images of people and houses in Jane Austen's fiction because she does not intend her prose to act primarily on our imagination.

Emily Brontë intends her novel to appeal to the reader's imagination; she uses language as a poet does. She often implies a connection between the natural world and the human:

'There's a little flower, up yonder, the last bud from the multitude of blue-bells . . . Will you clamber up, and pluck it to show to papa?'

Cathy stared a long time at the lonely blossom trembling in its earthy shelter, and replied, at length – 'No, I'll not touch it – but it looks melancholy, does it not, Ellen?' (Chapter 22)

This suggests the vulnerability of Cathy's position as the last of the Lintons and is typical of the method of the whole novel, where natural description and human character interact. In the same chapter we read:

> On an afternoon in October, or the beginning of November, a fresh
> watery afternoon, when the turf and paths were rustling with moist,
> withered leaves, and the cold, blue sky was half hidden by clouds –
> dark grey streamers, rapidly mounting from the west, and boding
> abundant rain – I requested my young lady to forego her ramble.

This sense of foreboding about the weather mirrors Edgar's imminent
death and his anxiety about what will become of Cathy.

With the compression of lyric poetry, Emily Brontë conveys through
a simple simile an idea that shapes our understanding of the novel:

> 'I've dreamt in my life dreams that have stayed with me ever after, and
> changed my ideas; they've gone through and through me, like wine
> through water, and altered the colour of my mind.' (Chapter 9)

We understand precisely what Catherine means when she says her
dreams 'altered the colour of my mind' though it would take pages to
spell it out in ordinary prose.

When Emily Brontë wants to suggest the mysteriousness of an intense
love she uses religious language, implying that the lovers operate or
communicate on a supernatural or at least inexplicable plane. Catherine
says that she has a sense of an existence beyond her own, which is
Heathcliff's, and he tells Ellen he cannot live without his soul, meaning
Catherine.

Theme

Wuthering Heights explores the nature of love and does not appear to
dismiss domestic love in favour of the intensity of the romantic
superhuman love of Heathcliff and Catherine. In the world of the novel
both can exist and the limitations of both are shown; Edgar, and his
daughter, when they are in love are sometimes trivial, but Heathcliff and
Catherine are self-obsessed and cruel. The final image we have of
Hareton and Cathy is a beautiful one, but they are to live in the Grange
because they do not belong to a world of exposed passions. Indeed they
are not passionate, though both are sensitive and loving.

The novel is not only about love; it also includes a variety of
suggestions about life after death and one does not eliminate another:
we are invited to speculate about it by Ellen, speaking of Catherine's
death.

> 'Do you believe such people *are* happy in the other world', sir? I'd give
> a great deal to know.'
>   I declined answering Mrs Dean's question, which struck me as
> something heterodox. (Chapter 16)

The novel itself is heterodox in that we feel that Heathcliff and Catherine attain their heaven, but that Edgar also reaches the peace he was searching for. The novel does seem to be about the incommunicable: the varieties of living, loving and dying which make up human experience. The impossibility of reducing the variety of human life to one strict code is shown in the character of Joseph; Emily Brontë suggests what she means to convey when Catherine says to Ellen: 'I can't do it distinctly – but I'll give you a feeling of how I feel.' (Chapter 9) The author gives us a feeling of how she feels by the welter of narrators in *Wuthering Heights*; instead of one controlling voice telling the story as in George Eliot's *Middlemarch* we hear the voices of Lockwood, Ellen, Heathcliff, Catherine, Zillah, Linton, Cathy and Isabella all narrating parts of the action and commenting on it.

The window image which recurs and is examined in detail in Part 4 reinforces this idea. We are constantly invited to look through windows with different characters and they become windows on experience, persuading us to look with the characters at a possible mode of being which we may not have considered before.

Achievement

The achievement of the book *Wuthering Heights* becomes clear if we see a film or television version of the novel. Without our reading the narrative accounts of Lockwood and Ellen the story can become crudely melodramatic. When we read the novel these two narrators root the extraordinary love of Heathcliff and Catherine in a credible realistic framework. Thus, because we recognise the real world, we are prepared to contemplate the spiritual world that Emily Brontë suggests exists beyond physical reality.

Emily Brontë's own view is hidden behind those of her many narrators; her technique as a novelist is oblique. We have to decide whether the ghosts of Heathcliff and Catherine could be in the Heights at the end, as three different views are suggested. The author's comment on her relationship with the reader might be reflected in Ellen's remark to Lockwood: 'But you'll not want to hear my moralising, Mr Lockwood: you'll judge as well as I can, all these things; at least, you'll think you will, and that's the same.' (Chapter 17)

Part 4

Hints for study

WE SHOULD NOW BE ABLE to answer the following questions:

(1) What is the most striking feature of the novel's structure?
(2) To what extent does the setting contribute to our understanding of the novel's theme?
(3) How do the vivid visual impressions the reader receives from *Wuthering Heights* help him to understand it?
(4) Why is the novel set in the past?
(5) What is unusual about the language of *Wuthering Heights*?
(6) Charlotte Brontë thought Heathcliff almost 'a man's shape animated by demon life – a Ghoul'. Do you agree?
(7) Is the last paragraph of the novel beautiful but totally misleading?
(8) Does the plot embody the meaning of the novel?
(9) 'Ellen Dean is the only sensible character in *Wuthering Heights* and we must trust her judgement.' Must we?
(10) Is *Wuthering Heights* a melodramatic novel?

The last three questions can be answered directly by briefly re-reading the sections on Melodrama, Narrative Method and Plot in Part 3.

Questions (1)—(5) require analysis of particular passages, and some relevant ones will be suggested; for questions (6) and (7) plans for possible answers will be given.

(1) The double narration is the most unusual feature of the novel's structure; Ellen is discussed in Narrative Method but the role of Lockwood needs detailed discussion. This can best be done by looking at the first three chapters and commenting on the following points:

  (*a*) Lockwood's pompous language compared with Heathcliff's directness.
  (*b*) His role as outsider, describing Yorkshire as a stranger to it.
  (*c*) His anecdote about his ludicrous love affair and his conceit about his own attractiveness; we feel he is a fool and we can trust his observation but not his judgement.
  (*d*) In Chapter 2 his incongruously elaborate language ('the favoured possessor of the beneficent fairy') compared with the brutality of the family; as readers we cannot sympathise with either.

(*e*) His dream, and the reduction of the civilised man to dragging the child's wrist brutally over the cut glass in the attempt to make the hand release his own: the channelling of our sympathy towards the young Catherine and Heathcliff.

(2) We sometimes understand what is happening to the characters through the use of setting; there are examples of this in the section on Setting (p. 44) here is one more: on the night that Heathcliff runs away in Chapter 9 there is a storm which splits off a tree. This is symbolic of what is happening to Heathcliff and Catherine and integrates them into the natural world.

(3) The novel is full of vivid views through windows; the section on Theme suggests their relation to the meaning of the novel.

(*a*) The ghost taps on the window at the beginning and Heathcliff is found dead by the same window at the end.

(*b*) The first time Heathcliff and Catherine see Thrushcross Grange they glimpse it through a window in Chapter 6. It is a vision of a different way of life; it is significant that the scene ends with Catherine as part of the interior and Heathcliff alone looking in from outside. It anticipates the future.

(*c*) Edgar and Catherine are sitting by an open window when Heathcliff returns from his exile in Chapter 10.

(*d*) Catherine leans out of a window at the Grange to try to see the Heights, catching the chill that kills her, in Chapter 12.

(*e*) Cathy climbs out of the window of her mother's old room, when she is imprisoned in the Heights, to get back to the Grange in Chapter 28.

(*f*) Lockwood looks in through a window at the Heights in the beautiful little scene when he sees Cathy and Hareton reading together, in Chapter 32.

(4) The novel is set within living memory of the time at which Emily Brontë wrote it, a common habit with Victorian novelists. It is not set so far in the past that it can be disregarded as historical fantasy, but by setting it a little in the past she introduces us to a rich folk tradition. The 'fairishes' that the characters believe in, and Ellen's ballads and superstitions create a suitable atmosphere for the ghosts, and enable the reader to dismiss this aspect of the book as old-fashioned nonsense if he wants to, as the civilised but stupid Lockwood does. Passages to include here are Ellen's ballads, for example in Chapter 9 and Catherine's vision of Ellen as a witch in Chapter 12.

(5) The vivid poetic quality of the language is its most remarkable

characteristic: the rhythm of the last paragraph for example and the ability to encapsulate something vital in a vigorous metaphor or simile.

(*a*) Everything that Catherine says in her scene with Ellen in Chapter 9 could be commented on but particularly these sentences: 'My love for Linton is like the foliage in the woods. Time will change it, I'm well aware, as winter changes the trees – my love for Heathcliff resembles the eternal rocks beneath – a source of little visible delight, but necessary.' This passage suggests the elemental quality of their love and shows how clearly she understands her own feelings.

(*b*) Cathy's account to Ellen in Chapter 10 of her idea of an ideal day and Linton Heathcliff's, brings the significant word 'heaven' into play again, and describes character through landscape.

(6) Essay plan for the question on Charlotte Brontë's attitude to Heathcliff. This view is taken from her Preface to the 1850 edition which most modern editions reproduce: it would be worth reading it in full first.

(*a*) Introduction – a summary of Charlotte Brontë's argument with perhaps a reference to other contemporary reviewers.

(*b*) Why does she think him a ghoul? Partly because of Ellen's attitude to him, and the number of times he is described as devilish, satanic, fiendish. Mr Earnshaw says he is as dark as if he came from the devil, etc. (References to make this point can be found throughout, but see Chapters 4 and 34 for examples of it.)

(*c*) Discussion of Ellen's reliability as a commentator on the action; she says she is superstitious, and we know she is steeped in folklore so she expects the child Heathcliff to be mysterious. The area of Yorkshire in which the novel is set is so enclosed that any stranger is suspect: see Ellen's response to Frances in Chapter 6.

(*d*) Comment on the way in which Emily Brontë makes Heathcliff credible as a character: we meet him first as a landlord then as a child before we come to his wilder actions. Even then details like the way he makes the tea in Chapter 27 prevent him from becoming fantastic.

From here the essay could develop in two ways. Either (*e*) into a discussion of Heathcliff's character showing that the ultimate moral responsibility for what happens rests with Catherine (see the sections on Time Scheme and Plot, and on Heathcliff's and Catherine's characters.) Or (*f*) into an analysis of Heathcliff as a romantic hero following the argument in the section on Heathcliff's character: that Heathcliff has the strengths of a passionate nature but also its accompanying ugliness and brutality. This would include a brief reference to the fact that

Catherine's betrayal of her true nature is partly what makes Heathcliff violent.

In this question a balance must be maintained; it is possible to make a defence of Heathcliff by qualifying his evil characteristics. Of course he, too, must take moral responsibility for his ill-treatment of Linton and Hareton, and for the possible murder of Hindley. Is Charlotte Brontë right when she says he is almost a ghoul, and that it is wrong to create such characters? If Heathcliff embodies a recognisable, if unusual, aspect of human experience then surely it is the business of literature to confront it.

(7) Essay plan for the question on the last paragraph:

(a) Is this passage beautiful? It requires close examination and comment on the use of evocative words like 'fluttering', and 'breathing' with its sense that the landscape is alive. The rhythm of the passage, created by the lengths of each part of the long sentence, is beautifully controlled in its movement from 'lingered' through 'watched' and 'listened' to 'wondered'. You could comment on the echoes some of the words have acquired in the course of the novel: 'heath' of course, and the 'hare-bells' remind us of Cathy's solitary bluebell in Chapter 22.

(b) This leads into discussion of 'sleepers in that quiet earth' and of Heathcliff's dream of 'sleeping the last sleep, by that sleeper' in Chapter 29. What did each of the three sleepers expect of death? Catherine thought it would eventually bring reunion with Heathcliff (Chapter 12); how can this be reconciled with Edgar's expectations in Chapter 28?

(c) Is this the final irony in the novel? One critic has said that the passage is ironic but that there is no evidence that Emily Brontë perceived the irony.* Could an artist as obviously aware of form as Emily Brontë is, lose control of the last paragraph? Is the point of the passage that the outsider, Lockwood, has failed to understand the story? He knows that the earth has not been quiet around Catherine's coffin but seems to ignore that, as Ellen does, in favour of a commonplace observation, about the dead being at peace.

(d) This should lead you into a general discussion of the roles of the two narrators, the ambiguity of the novel and the way in which Emily Brontë communicates with the reader through the narrators.

*Thomas Moser, 'Conflicting Impulses in *Wuthering Heights', Nineteenth Century Fiction*, Volume 17, No 1, June 1962

Part 5

Suggestions for further reading

The text

MARSDEN, HILDA AND JACK, IAN (ED.): *Wuthering Heights*, Clarendon Press, Oxford, 1976. The best modern text.

DAICHES, DAVID (ED.): *Wuthering Heights,* Penguin Books, Harmondsworth, 1965. Another good, easily available edition.

Biography

GASKELL, ELIZABETH: *The Life of Charlotte Brontë*, Smith, Elder & Co, London, 1857.

GERIN, WINIFRED: *Emily Brontë*, Clarendon Press, Oxford, 1971. A sympathetic contemporary account of the family.

Critical pieces

Critics have written stimulating but rather one-sided essays on *Wuthering Heights* so the most rewarding approach to reading criticism is likely to be by reading a collection of critical essays, to allow one critic to counterbalance the interpretation of another.

Two worthwhile collections are:

ALLOTT, MIRIAM (ED.): *Emily Brontë's 'Wuthering Heights'*, Macmillan Casebook, Macmillan, London, 1970.

SALE, WILLIAM M. (ED.): *Wuthering Heights, and Authoritative Text with Essays in Criticism*, W. W. Norton & Company, New York, 1963.

The author of these notes

ANGELA SMITH was educated and read English at the Universities of Birmingham and Cambridge. She has taught in Los Angeles and Wales and is now a lecturer in English Studies at the University of Stirling, where she has special responsibilities in the teaching of Commonwealth Literature. She has also worked part-time for the Open University since its inception.

York Notes: list of titles

CHINUA ACHEBE
A Man of the People
Arrow of God
Things Fall Apart

EDWARD ALBEE
Who's Afraid of Virginia Woolf?

ELECHI AMADI
The Concubine

ANONYMOUS
Beowulf
Everyman

AYI KWEI ARMAH
The Beautyful Ones Are Not Yet Born

W. H. AUDEN
Selected Poems

JANE AUSTEN
Emma
Mansfield Park
Northanger Abbey
Persuasion
Pride and Prejudice
Sense and Sensibility

HONORÉ DE BALZAC
Le Père Goriot

SAMUEL BECKETT
Waiting for Godot

SAUL BELLOW
Henderson, The Rain King

ARNOLD BENNETT
Anna of the Five Towns
The Card

WILLIAM BLAKE
Songs of Innocence, Songs of Experience

ROBERT BOLT
A Man For All Seasons

HAROLD BRIGHOUSE
Hobson's Choice

ANNE BRONTË
The Tenant of Wildfell Hall

CHARLOTTE BRONTË
Jane Eyre

EMILY BRONTË
Wuthering Heights

ROBERT BROWNING
Men and Women

JOHN BUCHAN
The Thirty-Nine Steps

JOHN BUNYAN
The Pilgrim's Progress

BYRON
Selected Poems

ALBERT CAMUS
L'Etranger (The Outsider)

GEOFFREY CHAUCER
Prologue to the Canterbury Tales
The Clerk's Tale
The Franklin's Tale
The Knight's Tale
The Merchant's Tale
The Miller's Tale
The Nun's Priest's Tale
The Pardoner's Tale
The Wife of Bath's Tale
Troilus and Criseyde

ANTON CHEKOV
The Cherry Orchard

SAMUEL TAYLOR COLERIDGE
Selected Poems

WILKIE COLLINS
The Moonstone

SIR ARTHUR CONAN DOYLE
The Hound of the Baskervilles

WILLIAM CONGREVE
The Way of the World

JOSEPH CONRAD
Heart of Darkness
Lord Jim
Nostromo
The Secret Agent
Victory
Youth and *Typhoon*

STEPHEN CRANE
The Red Badge of Courage

BRUCE DAWE
Selected Poems

WALTER DE LA MARE
Selected Poems

DANIEL DEFOE
A Journal of the Plague Year
Moll Flanders
Robinson Crusoe

CHARLES DICKENS
A Tale of Two Cities
Bleak House
David Copperfield
Dombey and Son
Great Expectations
Hard Times
Little Dorrit
Oliver Twist
Our Mutual Friend
The Pickwick Papers

EMILY DICKINSON
Selected Poems

JOHN DONNE
Selected Poems

JOHN DRYDEN
Selected Poems

GERALD DURRELL
My Family and Other Animals

GEORGE ELIOT
Adam Bede
Middlemarch
Silas Marner
The Mill on the Floss

T. S. ELIOT
Four Quartets
Murder in the Cathedral
Selected Poems
The Cocktail Party
The Waste Land

J. G. FARRELL
The Siege of Krishnapur

GEORGE FARQUHAR
The Beaux Stratagem

WILLIAM FAULKNER
Absalom, Absalom!
The Sound and the Fury

HENRY FIELDING
Joseph Andrews
Tom Jones

F. SCOTT FITZGERALD
Tender is the Night
The Great Gatsby

GUSTAVE FLAUBERT
Madame Bovary

E. M. FORSTER
A Passage to India
Howards End

JOHN FOWLES
The French Lieutenant's Woman

ATHOL FUGARD
Selected Plays

JOHN GALSWORTHY
Strife

MRS GASKELL
North and South

WILLIAM GOLDING
Lord of the Flies
The Spire

OLIVER GOLDSMITH
She Stoops to Conquer
The Vicar of Wakefield

ROBERT GRAVES
Goodbye to All That

GRAHAM GREENE
Brighton Rock
The Heart of the Matter
The Power and the Glory

WILLIS HALL
The Long and the Short and the Tall

THOMAS HARDY
Far from the Madding Crowd
Jude the Obscure
Selected Poems
Tess of the D'Urbervilles
The Mayor of Casterbridge
The Return of the Native
The Trumpet Major
The Woodlanders
Under the Greenwood Tree

L. P. HARTLEY
The Go-Between
The Shrimp and the Anemone

NATHANIEL HAWTHORNE
The Scarlet Letter

SEAMUS HEANEY
Selected Poems

JOSEPH HELLER
Catch-22

ERNEST HEMINGWAY
A Farewell to Arms
For Whom the Bell Tolls
The Old Man and the Sea

GEORGE HERBERT
Selected Poems

HERMANN HESSE
Steppenwolf

BARRY HINES
Kes

HOMER
The Iliad
The Odyssey

ANTHONY HOPE
The Prisoner of Zenda

GERARD MANLEY HOPKINS
Selected Poems

WILLIAM DEAN HOWELLS
The Rise of Silas Lapham

RICHARD HUGHES
A High Wind in Jamaica

TED HUGHES
Selected Poems

THOMAS HUGHES
Tom Brown's Schooldays

ALDOUS HUXLEY
Brave New World

HENRIK IBSEN
A Doll's House
Ghosts

HENRY JAMES
Daisy Miller
The Ambassadors
The Europeans
The Portrait of a Lady
The Turn of the Screw
Washington Square

SAMUEL JOHNSON
Rasselas

BEN JONSON
The Alchemist
Volpone

JAMES JOYCE
A Portrait of the Artist as a Young Man
Dubliners

JOHN KEATS
Selected Poems

RUDYARD KIPLING
Kim

D. H. LAWRENCE
Sons and Lovers
The Rainbow
Women in Love

CAMARA LAYE
L'Enfant Noir

HARPER LEE
To Kill a Mocking-Bird

LAURIE LEE
Cider with Rosie

THOMAS MANN
Tonio Kröger

CHRISTOPHER MARLOWE
Doctor Faustus

ANDREW MARVELL
Selected Poems

W. SOMERSET MAUGHAM
Selected Short Stories

GAVIN MAXWELL
Ring of Bright Water

J. MEADE FALKNER
Moonfleet

HERMAN MELVILLE
Billy Budd
Moby Dick

THOMAS MIDDLETON
Women Beware Women

THOMAS MIDDLETON *and* WILLIAM ROWLEY
The Changeling

ARTHUR MILLER
A View from the Bridge
Death of a Salesman
The Crucible

JOHN MILTON
Paradise Lost I & II
Paradise Lost IV & IX
Selected Poems

V. S. NAIPAUL
A House for Mr Biswas

ROBERT O'BRIEN
Z for Zachariah

SEAN O'CASEY
Juno and the Paycock

GABRIEL OKARA
The Voice

EUGENE O'NEILL
Mourning Becomes Electra

GEORGE ORWELL
Animal Farm
Nineteen Eighty-four

JOHN OSBORNE
Look Back in Anger

WILFRED OWEN
Selected Poems

ALAN PATON
Cry, The Beloved Country

THOMAS LOVE PEACOCK
Nightmare Abbey and *Crotchet Castle*

HAROLD PINTER
The Caretaker

PLATO
The Republic

ALEXANDER POPE
Selected Poems

J. B. PRIESTLEY
An Inspector Calls

THOMAS PYNCHON
The Crying of Lot 49

SIR WALTER SCOTT
Ivanhoe
Quentin Durward
The Heart of Midlothian
Waverley

PETER SHAFFER
The Royal Hunt of the Sun

WILLIAM SHAKESPEARE
A Midsummer Night's Dream
Antony and Cleopatra
As You Like It
Coriolanus
Cymbeline
Hamlet
Henry IV Part I
Henry IV Part II
Henry V
Julius Caesar
King Lear
Love's Labour's Lost
Macbeth
Measure for Measure
Much Ado About Nothing
Othello
Richard II
Richard III
Romeo and Juliet
Sonnets
The Merchant of Venice
The Taming of the Shrew
The Tempest
The Winter's Tale
Troilus and Cressida
Twelfth Night

GEORGE BERNARD SHAW
Androcles and the Lion
Arms and the Man
Caesar and Cleopatra
Candida
Major Barbara
Pygmalion
Saint Joan
The Devil's Disciple

MARY SHELLEY
Frankenstein

PERCY BYSSHE SHELLEY
Selected Poems

RICHARD BRINSLEY SHERIDAN
The School for Scandal
The Rivals

R. C. SHERRIFF
Journey's End

WOLE SOYINKA
The Road
Three Short Plays

EDMUND SPENSER
The Faerie Queene (Book I)

JOHN STEINBECK
Of Mice and Men
The Grapes of Wrath
The Pearl

LAURENCE STERNE
A Sentimental Journey
Tristram Shandy

ROBERT LOUIS STEVENSON
Kidnapped
Treasure Island
Dr Jekyll and Mr Hyde

TOM STOPPARD
Professional Foul
Rosencruntz and Guildenstern are Dead

JONATHAN SWIFT
Gulliver's Travels

JOHN MILLINGTON SYNGE
The Playboy of the Western World

TENNYSON
Selected Poems

W. M. THACKERAY
Vanity Fair

DYLAN THOMAS
Under Milk Wood

EDWARD THOMAS
Selected Poems

FLORA THOMPSON
Lark Rise to Candleford

J. R. R. TOLKIEN
The Hobbit
The Lord of the Rings

ANTHONY TROLLOPE
Barchester Towers

MARK TWAIN
Huckleberry Finn
Tom Sawyer

JOHN VANBRUGH
The Relapse

VIRGIL
The Aeneid

VOLTAIRE
Candide

KEITH WATERHOUSE
Billy Liar

EVELYN WAUGH
Decline and Fall

JOHN WEBSTER
The Duchess of Malfi
The White Devil

H. G. WELLS
The History of Mr Polly
The Invisible Man
The War of the Worlds

OSCAR WILDE
The Importance of Being Earnest

THORNTON WILDER
Our Town

TENNESSEE WILLIAMS
The Glass Menagerie

VIRGINIA WOOLF
Mrs Dalloway
To the Lighthouse

WILLIAM WORDSWORTH
Selected Poems

WILLIAM WYCHERLEY
The Country Wife

W. B. YEATS
Selected Poems